W9-BGR-263

PRAISE FOR
THE CHILD QUEEN

"THE CHILD QUEEN is a lovely story, a wonderfully human retelling of the Arthur and Guinevere legend, one touched with passion and enchantment."
—JENNIFER BLAKE

"A tale of enchantment. A love story like no other. You will be charmed. Surely Merlin's magic reached out to touch Nancy McKenzie's pen. Ms. McKenzie weaves a rich and powerful tapestry of words layered in legend and myth. Sit back and enjoy, for who of us would not wish to return to Camelot? Nancy McKenzie is going places!"
—ELAINE COFFMAN

"Guinevere comes alive—a strong, resourceful, and compassionate woman, accessible to modern folk . . . McKenzie makes a quantum leap in defining the character of Guinevere as a real, flesh-and-blood woman. The Arthur-Guinevere-Lancelot triangle comes alive as well—believable, poignant, and bearing the seeds of tragedy. Nancy McKenzie is truly an important discovery of the year! My congratulations!"
—KATHERINE KURTZ

Look for these Del Rey Discoveries . . .
Because something new is always worth the risk!

DEMON DRUMS by Carol Severance
THE QUICKSILVER SCREEN by Don H. DeBrandt
A PLAGUE OF CHANGE by L. Warren Douglas
CHILDREN OF THE EARTH by Catherine Wells
THE OUTSKIRTER'S SECRET by Rosemary Kirstein
MIND LIGHT by Margaret Davis
AMMONITE by Nicola Griffith
DANCER OF THE SIXTH by Michelle Shirey Crean
THE DRYLANDS by Mary Rosenblum
McLENDON'S SYNDROME by Robert Frezza
BRIGHT ISLANDS IN A DARK SEA by L. Warren Douglas
THE RISING OF THE MOON by Flynn Connolly
CHIMERA by Mary Rosenblum
THE IMPERIUM GAME by K. D. Wentworth
THE HELDAN by Debroah Talmadge-Bickmore
MISTWALKER by Denise Lopes Heald
THE CHILD QUEEN by Nancy McKenzie

THE CHILD QUEEN

THE TALE OF GUINEVERE AND KING ARTHUR

NANCY MCKENZIE

A Del Rey® Book
BALLANTINE BOOKS • NEW YORK

A Del Rey® Book
Published by Ballantine Books

Library of Congress Catalog Card Number: 94-94192

ISBN 0-345-38244-7

Manufactured in the United States of America

First Edition: August 1994

10 9 8 7 6 5 4 3 2 1

To Meg and Bruce

Anyone who has ever read any one of Mary Stewart's Merlin trilogy (*The Crystal Cave, The Hollow Hills, The Last Enchantment*) will know how much I owe to her vision of fifth-century Britain. These books, among others, inspired me to create my own tale about Guinevere, Arthur, Lancelot, and the real world these legendary people inhabit. I am indebted to many who have contributed to the Arthurian tradition, historians and storytellers alike. As I have built upon the works of others, so I hope some future writer might build upon mine. After all, that is the ultimate compliment—to be considered even a small part of the tradition surrounding this ancient, time-tested tale.

Special thanks are due to several people whose help and encouragement are directly responsible for the publication of this book. Meg Gossmann, my sister and first reader, went to a lot of trouble to convince me to find an agent; Bruce McKenzie, my husband, gave me the courage to try; Virginia Kidd, my agent, gave me good advice and dealt patiently with my questions; and Deborah Hogan, my editor, worked long and hard to give my story shape.

I thank also my friend Kate Delaney for her gift of Xenophon's *On Horsemanship*, and John Downey of the Andrus Planetarium, The Hudson River Museum, for his prompt answers to astronomical questions. Karen Kramer gave me invaluable support and advice about writing and editing; Caroline McKenzie helped me research White and Malory; Marsha Gorelick and Lydia Soifer provided me a constant source of excited and enthusiastic support, and Joellen Finnie listened patiently to hours of what must have been, in retrospect, boring detail.

I thank all of you for making this possible.

Nancy McKenzie
November, 1993

Arthur's Britain

Map by S.F. Palmer

PROLOGUE

The night of my birth the famed witch Giselda, the ugliest woman in all Britain, came to see my father, the King of Northgallis. It was the last night in April, cold and blowing a fine, icy rain. My father and his drinking companions, such nobles and petty lords as could leave their lands in the hands of others, sat in the hall before a great log fire while the women attended my mother and brought him tidings as the night wore on.

The guard let her in, not knowing who she was. She was old and bent, her hands were crippled and swollen, and my father's hospitality to the poor and infirm was well known. But she would not stay to warm herself before the peat fire in the kitchen, where the cooks were heating water for the queen's birthing. She made for the hall and the king. When the guard would have stopped her, she lifted her hood and glared at him. The very sight of her face froze him to the spot where he stood, and she passed by.

Likewise, when she came into the hall, and the company turned to her in surprise and then protest, she silenced them all when she uncovered her head.

"King Leodegrance!" she cried.

My father faced her. He was always the bravest man among brave men. "I am he, witch. State your business and be gone. You come at a time of celebration, and we would not be interrupted! Know you not my young queen gives birth this night?" His companions cheered him, and he even smiled at the old witch. He was the father of five sons of fighting age and the new husband of the loveliest woman in Wales. He could afford to be magnanimous.

But the witch stared at him, trancelike, until the room was quiet and all eyes were on her. "Beware, King! Laugh not until the night is over! It is a night of wonders! The queenstar in the east has fallen in a hail of light. And in its place burns a new star of wondrous brightness! The fairest in the heavens! These are portents of things to come. There is magic in the air this night. In this house."

My father was not a Christian, nor were the others in the room. He worshipped Mithra, the Bull-Slayer, when he was at war, along with all the other men who fought under the High King Uther Pendragon, and the Great Goddess when he was at peace. Yet he also believed in the ancient gods of his ancestors, the gods of roadways and rivers, of the storm winds, the low forests and the high hills, gods whom men had worshipped before ever the Romans came to Britain. To speak to him of magic was to touch him near the heart, and he was afraid.

"What do you mean, woman?" he demanded, hiding his fear in anger. "Where in this house?"

The witch grinned, showing black and broken teeth. Her voice fell into a low and vibrant monotone, and all strained to hear her words. "This night shall be born a daughter who shall rule the mightiest in the land." Her words fell on silence. The king, my father, stared. "She will be the fairest beauty the world has known and the highest lady in all the kingdoms of Britain. Her name will live on in the minds of men for ages to come. Through her will you reach glory." Here she paused and passed her tongue over dry, cracked lips. Someone handed her a cup of spiced wine, and she drank. "But she will bring you pain, King, before ever she brings you joy. Beloved of kings, she shall betray a king and be herself betrayed. Hers will be a fate no one will envy. She will be the white shadow over the brightest glory of Britain." Here she stopped, shook herself awake, and, doing my stunned father a low curtsy, hurried out of the house before any man had sense enough to stop her.

The room was at once alive with voices. Each man asked his neighbor what she had meant. Each man thought he knew what the prophecy foretold. All of them took it as wonderful news for my father, except my father himself. He sat frowning in his great chair, saying over and over "the white shadow. White shadow." He used the Celtic word the witch had spoken: *gwenhwyfar*.

Just before dawn the weather broke, and the wind softened. It was the first of May, a day sacred to the ancient Goddess, and the queen's labors were over. My father, asleep over his wine like his fellows, awoke with a start of premonition to find his chamberlain trembling at his elbow. He was charged with a dolorous message.

The good Queen Elen had brought forth a daughter, but had died thereof. With her last breath she had kissed me, and named me: Guinevere.

1 ✹ NORThGALLIS

My seventh year was my last one at home. It was not customary in those days for boys and girls of noble birth to spend their youth as pages and ladies-in-waiting in strangers' castles. Those were troubled times. The land was not at peace, and men did not trust one another. The law lay in the strongest sword. Outlaws lived among the hills, making travel treacherous. Even warriors undertook journeys only upon necessity, and that usually meant war.

And to tell truth, there were not many real "castles" in Wales. Our strongest buildings were fighting fortresses, where the king's troops slept on straw strewn over dirt flooring, and the walls of dressed stone were unadorned by the tapestries and weavings that kept the wind from our cozy rooms at home in the king's house. Caer Narvon, on our northern border, was the biggest fortress in Wales. It had been built by the Romans and then left to decay with the passing of centuries, but it was still in use as a fighting fortress and was our securest defense against the Irish raiders. With Y Wyddfa, the Snow Mountain, at its rear, and the Western Sea under its guarding eye, it was considered impregnable and was the pride of all Wales.

Nowadays, every petty king has a wonderful castle of quarried stone and plenty of tapestries and fine silks and cushions and carpets to adorn it, for the land has been at peace for twenty years and we have all had time, blessed time, to devote to the arts of peace. But in my childhood, the king's house was a simple enough dwelling. Welshmen have a devilish pride, and even the king's house could not outshine his soldiers' homes by much, else he have trouble on his hands.

My father's house at Cameliard was of wood and wattle, with a large meeting and drinking hall that had a hole cut in the roof to let out the firesmoke. Beautiful hangings adorned the walls, keeping out the winter winds, and beneath the fresh rushes on the floor were real Roman tiles. Cracked and faded as they were, the designs were still discernible. I remember a crouching panther, birds with bright feathers and long necks, and a golden lion, seated and serene, which was just in front of my chair, next to my father on the dais. He kept me by him all the time; I believe he was very lonely. During long audiences and even meetings with his men, I was beside him and amused myself by watching the animals on the floor and imagining that they moved and spoke. The men never bothered about me. They assumed I could understand nothing of their schemes and worries, and I never undeceived them.

Indeed, growing up without a mother had a few definite advantages. Instead of spending all my time with the queen's waiting women, learning needlework and the weaving of war cloaks, I was allowed to go where I would, with either my nurse Ailsa or some page of the king's as companion. I rode everywhere. In my youth, horses gave me freedom and independence; later, they were my comfort and solace. I have taken this to be a sign from God, that I should live in close harmony with these most honored of his creatures. With sturdy Welsh mountain ponies as my friends and teachers in childhood, I grew bold and free and as wild, they said, as any boy. Which is how, in the autumn of my seventh year, I caused trouble, lost my best friend, and learned an important lesson about friendship and power.

The king my father and all his sons and all their attendants were away on a boar hunt. Every year at the change in seasons, the king took his sport, and the men brought back venison and boar to be salted away for palace feasts all winter.

In the village women gathered the harvest of their gardens and small plots, foraged for berries and late herbs, prepared flax for winter's weaving and dyes for winter dyeing. Men went hunting, from the king and his courtiers down to the lowliest peasant; all the animals of the forests throughout Wales took heed; waterfowl fell to men's nets in the marshes, and fish to nets in the lakes and hill ponds. Everyone was busy, even the children. But as royal children, my cousins and I had it easier than most. We collected windfalls from the palace orchards, and when the gardeners were done with their other duties, we scrambled into the trees and shook off the ripening fruit for them to collect in their woven baskets.

I speak of my cousins, who were my playmates in these early

days, but actually they were my nephews. My father's sons by his first wife, Gwella, were grown men, with children of their own. My eldest brother, Gwarthgydd, was seven and twenty, a thick, powerful man with a thatch of black hair on his head and a mat of hair nearly as thick on his body. Most children feared him for his temper, but he had a ready smile and kind heart and was always good to me. His youngest son, Gwillim, was only a year older than me and was my best friend. There were not many girls in our family, and none of them was kind to me, for I did not look much like them, but took after my mother. Gwill's two older sisters were my chief tormenters. They insulted the memory of my mother, the affection of my father, whom I adored, the frailty of my body, which was not thick and dark and sturdy like their own, even the pale color of my hair, as if I could change it of my will. In my innocence, I did not understand it.

On a fine autumn day in the month of the Raven, Gwillim and I could not resist the chance to sneak away from work, only for an hour, to play in the wooded hills that encircled our valley. We pretended we were hunters, tracking our prey along the winding banks of a brook that led up through the hills to a spring in a mossy clearing. There we would flop on our stomachs to rest, drinking the clear water and pouring a small libation for the god of the place, for everyone knew that springs were holy. We could see the white shoulders of Y Wyddfa, the highest mountain in Wales, from that clearing. Its peak was always shrouded in mist, for gods lived there.

Sometimes, when I beat Gwill to the clearing, he would complain that I was cheating, for I was a girl and shouldn't have been there at all. Instead of a gown, I wore soft doeskin leggings better than his own, and as I was taller and my legs were longer than his, I ran faster and was more adept. He didn't really hold these things against me—he liked the challenge. But he disliked being taunted by his brothers and cousins that he played with girls and would grow up to be one. I don't blame him; they were cruel taunts, and I loved him more because he defended me to my enemies and took their abuse for my sake.

This day he reached the clearing first and was already on his knees pouring the libation when I arrived. We knelt together, mumbled our thanks to the god, and drank. Then we sat side by side and gazed at the distant heights of Y Wyddfa, which sparkled in the afternoon sun.

"Gwen, do you think anybody has ever seen a god?" he asked suddenly.

"Of course," I replied in surprise. "Holy men talk with them. Magicians and witches command them. They are everywhere, all about."

"Yes," he said slowly, his eyes on the mountain. "So men say. But if they are everywhere, why can't we see them?"

I was puzzled by his obtuseness. "Because you need special powers to see them," I patiently explained. "That's what makes holy men holy."

"Exactly," he said, turning to me eagerly. "What makes them holy is that they can see and talk to gods. But they can't see and talk to gods unless they are holy. You see?"

"See what?"

"Who's to prove or disprove it? It's their claim to be holy that makes them so. If I claim to be a wizard, it's my claim that makes me powerful, for no one can disprove that I talk to spirits."

"Gwill, do you mean that you don't—you don't believe in gods?"

"No. Of course not. Didn't we just pray to one? I mean, well—my mother fears a witch's curse because she believes the witch has power, and it's her believing that the witch has power that gives her the power she fears. Do you see?"

I was very impressed with his reasoning. But I had a more practical mind. "What witch has cursed her? What did she say?"

He looked a little embarrassed, and I guessed that he was not supposed to tell anyone.

"Swear by Mithra the foul fates," he commanded, and I solemnly swore by Mithra to bring devastation upon myself and my family and my descendants if ever a word that Gwill confided to me should pass my lips.

"Well," he said more easily, "Haggar of the Hills came by in the guise of a beggar as my mother and sisters were washing at the brook. She begged a drink of honey mead that they carried in their flask, for she was thirsty and dusty. Mother pointed out that the brook water was good enough for such as she, and my sisters claimed that common folk would fall ill drinking the mead of the royal house."

I grinned. Gwillim thought his mother insufferably snobbish about her connection to the royal house. Glynis had been the daughter of one of my father's minor nobles and not a good match for Gwarthgydd, but she had been lovely when young, and he had stood by her and married her when she got with child. In return for his kindness, she lorded her position over everyone around her and made everyone's life miserable if she could.

Someday, no doubt, if Gwarth lived, she would be queen, and she let no one forget it. But for all that, Gwill was devoted to her, and often rose well before dawn to fish the stream for speckled trout, which she adored. He was her favorite. All his transgressions she forgave him.

"Then Haggar revealed herself and called upon the powers of the air. My sisters say the sky darkened, but I do not believe this. I was not far away that day, and I saw nothing. She cursed my mother's vanity, saying that the highest shall be brought low and the least valued made high; that all my mother's hopes should come to naught, and her line should dwindle. That her home should be destroyed, and her husband die in a far-off land." He gulped and continued. "And that the Kingdom of Northgallis should be swallowed by a great dragon and disappear from the face of the earth forever."

I stared at him in horror. "Northgallis disappear?" I whispered. "Oh, Gwillim, no! What does it mean? Saxons?"

He shook his head. He was clearly more worried about the fate of his family than about the Kingdom of Northgallis. "Don't you see what my mother has done? She made the old woman mad, and now she believes every word she said. But what if the old woman isn't really a witch? I mean, what if everybody just thinks she is? Nothing need come to pass unless we make it so by believing it will."

I gazed at him with wonder and respect. "You are the bravest boy I know, Gwillim, son of Gwarthgydd. To think you can save Northgallis simply by believing you can—it's wonderful. Does this mean that the witch has no power over you?"

He flushed with pleasure and smiled. "She doesn't determine my future, Gwen, unless I believe that she does. That's what I think."

"And—and is this true also of other witches? And enchanters? What about the High King's enchanter? What about Merlin?"

He shivered at the name of the great magician, but bravely stuck to his belief. "Yes, it is also true of Merlin. But—but perhaps I might believe Merlin," he admitted, frowning. "He is wise as well as powerful. He is not afraid of kings."

The air around us had gone very still. The fleecy clouds hung motionless in the sky, and the birds fell silent in the trees. I realized suddenly that we were talking in whispers, and a thrill of foreboding ran up my spine.

"And the gods?" I breathed, wide-eyed. "Are they the same? Have they power only over those who worship them, so that

Mithra has power over warriors, and the Elder spirits over the common people and the hill people, and the new *Kyrios Christos* over the Christians?"

He stared at me. We hardly dared to breathe in the awful silence.

"You understand me," he whispered, and we were filled with terror at our sacrilege.

Suddenly we were not alone in the clearing; we felt the new presence before we heard or saw anything. For an instant time stood still, and we saw in each other's eyes the everlasting terror of perdition. Then I saw behind him, at the edge of the clearing, the soft brown eyes and pink nose of a wild mountain pony, and I exhaled with relief. We were not to be claimed by spirits after all! A small band of ponies had come to the spring to drink, that was all. Gwill turned slowly, flushing scarlet when he saw them, four of them, edging daintily toward the spring pool. We sat still, and they gathered courage and came forward, three of them lowering their pretty heads to drink, while the fourth eyed us warily.

Gwill was ashamed of his terror and needed to feel brave.

"They're very fine," he said softly. "And the leader is black. That's very rare. Let's see if we can catch two."

I was entranced. Ever since my father had placed me himself on a fat little pony at the age of three, I had loved horses. They spoke a language I somehow understood, and riding came effortlessly to me. At seven, I was already as good a rider as boys of eleven and twelve, who were ready for war training. And while Gwill was only slightly less skilled than I, catching wild ponies was a very different thing from riding trained ones and was a job for a group of mounted men and not for two children.

Nevertheless, I assented immediately and drew from my belt the windfalls I had brought along for our hunter's meal. Keeping movement to a minimum, I approached the nearest pony, a white one, offering the apple. While the other ponies scented danger and backed away, this one was overcome by curiosity and showed no fear. I fed him the apple and stroked his neck, lifting the heavy mane and scratching his withers. His eyes closed with pleasure, and Gwill whispered "Now!" In a single leap I was astride. The pony snorted in fear, spun around, and tore off through the woods. I buried my fists in his mane and clung to him for dear life, lying low on his back as we crashed through the brush, and branches whipped at my face and hair. I had a vague picture of Gwill grappling with the black one, his belt around its neck, but I could hear nothing behind me. The other ponies had bolted, too, but whether

Gwill was with them I had no idea. I spoke to the terrified pony in a low singsong, as we Welsh do, hoping he could hear me over the clatter of his hooves. Eventually he slowed, either calmed by the song or tired from his fruitless efforts. He cantered, then trotted, then came to a trembling halt. I stroked and comforted him but did not dismount. I let him feel my legs against his sides, gently, and then I sat up. As he got over his fear, he seemed to understand the messages my legs and body sent him. It is magic of a sort, speaking to horses, and a thrill I have never outgrown. We walked along a woodland track until he was calm and had got his breath back. Then, crooning to him all the while, I headed him back the way we had come, as well as I could judge. He was lathered with fear and sweat, his sides were slippery. So when, as we neared the spring, I heard my name suddenly shouted from the top of the ridge and the pony reared in fright, I slipped off as quickly as a raindrop from a downspout and fell hard against a tree. The last thing I remembered was the cry "Guinevere!" echoing among the hills, and then the world went black.

I began to hear voices, dimly, as if from a distance. I was warm and protected deep in my darkness, and the voices washed over me in gentle swells, gently rolling me this way and that. I was tired, too tired to move, so I lay still and listened to the coming and going of the voices.

Gradually I floated nearer the bright surface, and the voices came more clearly. There was a kind, deep voice that spoke in quiet desperation, and a higher-pitched voice that spat in angry whispers.

"It's not fair!" came the angry voice. "He has no right to kill the boy!"

"He has the right of the king," the deep voice replied slowly, wearily. "And he will not do it if she lives. So do your job and nurse her, Glynis. Enough of this argument."

"You listen to me, Gwarth! This girl is a curse to your house, to your family, and to your line. She was cursed on the night of her birth by the most powerful witch in Wales, do you not remember?"

"Hush, woman!"

Glynis lowered her voice, but her spite intensified. "She has brought nothing but trouble to Northgallis since that day. She killed her mother the queen with her birth. We had drought in her first year of life and a killing frost in her second. She is spoiled and petted by all the king's courtiers and servants. Even you! Yes,

even you, with fine children of your own, are kinder to her than
to them. She is a young witch, I tell you—"

"Woman, I will put you away! Hold your tongue!"

"She has woven a spell around Gwillim. He is enchanted, I tell
you! He follows her everywhere! And now, a week after the hill
witch's curse—"

"By the Bull! I am tired of hearing about that hag—"

"She said my house would be destroyed and my line dimin-
ished! And now this! This—this brazen witch leads my son into
the hills, gets herself hurt, and now the king your father will take
his life in vengeance! If that isn't diminishing my line, what is!
Gwarth, he is your son, too! Can't you stop it?"

The deep voice came nearer; it was very kind. "Glynis. Calm
yourself. Do your duty and poultice the girl. She is only a child.
This was an accident, my dear. Children are heir to them. She can
do you no harm unless she dies. You have seen your own children
recover from worse falls than this."

"Yes," Glynis continued, her fury unabated, "but they were
strong children, not dainty and pampered like this one. If it were
not for Gwillim, I would not try to save her! Oh, gods!" she cried,
choking. "Tell me, why does everyone love her so much?"

Gwarth was silent while Glynis sobbed noisily. "She is ugly!"
she blurted. "Such fairness—such pallor—is ugly! Her bones are
too small! She cannot work; she is useless! My daughters are
more worthy to be princesses of Northgallis! They are strong,
and—and . . . they are brown and healthy . . . I hate her! I hate
her!"

She must have sensed she had gone too far, for she began to
mumble an apology and flung a cloth across my brow.

For a long time Gwarthgydd said nothing. Then he spoke with
the voice of command. "*You* have destroyed your house. *You* will
diminish your line. I put you away. Take your brown daughters
with you, Glynis, and go."

The woman screamed, and pain shot through my head. I pulled
the quiet darkness around me with thanks and sank into its depths.

When I awoke it was early evening. I was in my own bedchamber, and a wood fire burned in the grate. The king's physician sat by my side, watching me eagerly. I was wrapped in warm
furs, and my head was bound in cool cloth. When I looked about
me, the outlines of things were murky, but soon my sight cleared,
and the physician uttered a prayer of thanks to Mithra.

I knew what I must do.

"Where is my father?" I asked him. "Is the king near? Bring him to me."

The physician nodded and patted my hand soothingly. "King Leodegrance is but waiting for word of your awakening." He snapped his fingers, and the page by the door hurried out. The physician poured some warm broth into a flat bowl and supported my head while I drank of it. It tasted of herbs and medicines, but it was warming and steadied my head.

"Please help me to sit up," I begged, but the physician insisted I lie quietly.

"If my father is coming, I will sit up," I commanded, using the voice I heard Gwarthgydd use, and the physician obeyed immediately. I was dizzy and my head felt several sizes too large, but I could hold myself erect.

"How long have I been here?"

"Since yesterday, my lady. You were brought to me in the evening."

"Please tell me what happened before the king comes. It is important that I know. I remember nothing of it."

He hesitated, but gave in to me. "When the king's hunting party returned, the palace was in an uproar because you could not be found. No one remembered having seen you since midday. In fear of their lives, the gardeners and house servants took to the hills to look for you."

"And Gwillim," I added, but he averted his eyes. "Yes, my lady. Ailsa fell down in a fit with brain fever. She is delirious still." Ailsa, my nurse, was a loving but lazy soul, who had attended me from birth. It was during one of her illicit naps in the garden that I had stolen away.

"I expect she will recover when she finds out I am all right."

The physician was doubtful. "It appears to be a serious case, my lady."

"Never mind. I will cure her. How did you find me? What of Gwillim?"

He looked uncomfortable when I said his name, and I began to be afraid.

"The king's son Gwarthgydd and his men found you, coming down from the hills across the back of a white pony, led by Gwillim," the physician said, frowning. "The lad was frantic. He thought you were dead. He told King Leodegrance he had led you away from the orchard and taken you to play with him in the hills. He said you had seen some wild ponies, and he dared you to catch one. He blamed himself for what happened. He said it was punishment for evil thoughts."

"Did the king believe him?" I whispered.

"We all believed him, my lady."

"And where is he now? Pray, quick! I hear the guards!"

"He is—he is in the king's dungeon, my lady. His family is disgraced."

"It was not his fault!" I cried hotly, but cut off my speech, for the door swung open, and my dear father strode into the room.

"Gwen!" He took me gently into his arms, and I hugged him and kissed his rough cheek. "Praise Mithra you are alive! How do you feel? Shouldn't you be lying down?"

"Not yet," I said, to forestall the physician. "I must speak with you first, dear Father. Can I see you alone?"

A wave of his hand sent the others out of the room, although the physician did not like to go.

"Father," I said, looking right into his eyes. "I owe my life to Gwillim. He saved me when I fell, and he brought me home. If it were not for Gwillim, I would be with Mother now. Can you send him to me, that I may thank him?"

The reference to my mother diffused his rising anger, and he grumbled a bit. "That is not what Gwillim says," he objected. "He admits that he endangered your life. He didn't claim he saved you."

I managed a blush and took his big, brown, callused hand between my own small white ones. "Well, what would you expect him to say? That your daughter behaved like an Irish hooligan? That she enticed him away from his chores and ran off to the hills to enjoy the day, knowing he would be forced to escort her? That she bragged she could catch and ride a wild pony, although he begged her not to risk it? And that when she was thrown and lay senseless, he found her and managed to tame the wild pony himself and bring her home upon its back? Would you have believed such a story?"

He glowered at me. "No, I would not. And I do not believe it now."

I sighed and inwardly took a deep breath. "Well, my dearest father, it is near the truth. I have behaved very badly, toward you and toward Gwillim. I humbly ask your forgiveness. I was thoughtless and selfish. I have caused Gwillim to lie to defend my honor, and I am ashamed."

He looked at me searchingly, but I withstood him. His uncertainty gave way at last to resignation. "Do you swear by the blood of the Bull this is the truth?"

"I swear it."

"Well," he said at length, "I am both grieved and relieved to hear it. I will send Gwillim to you after I have spoken to him, and when the physician says I may. You should be punished, Guinevere; but it is not in me to do it. And indeed, I believe Mithra will see to it in his own way, and in his own time."

"There is one other thing." He was getting up to go, and he turned warily, scenting deception. I put on the most guileless face I could summon.

"May I also have my nurse back? I dislike this physician near me. In my illness, I remember a light touch that comforted me. Would it be possible to send her back to me?"

He looked confused, but could not resist my supplication. "If you mean Glynis, she is gone from the house." As the ranking woman, after me, of the royal house, Gwarthgydd's wife would be appointed nurse to any royal patient.

"If she is gone because of Gwillim, can it not be put right?"

The king stood and looked down full upon me. "Guinevere, are you asking me to send you that jealous shrew? Do you really want her with you? Are your wits about you? You needn't— Gwillim is safe without that."

Safe, perhaps, but miserable and forever shamed without his mother. I trembled with the effort it cost me, but I lied. "She is a good nurse."

He stared at me and then shook his head. "All right. She is yours. But when you are well, my girl, you and I must talk about your future."

"Yes, Father," I said meekly.

Glynis returned the next morning. Her face was rough and blotched with the marks of blows and tears, and I guessed that Gwarth had lost his temper once again. There was no love in her face, no understanding, no gratitude; only fear. I was a witch; she was beholden to me, and she was afraid. I did not speak to her, but let her tend me and feed me with what tenderness she could muster, and we got along tolerably well.

In the evening Gwillim was brought to my door. Glynis would have embraced him, but Gwillim kept his eyes on the floor, and she crept out without a word.

I lay on the pillows and looked at Gwillim. He would not look at me. He was newly washed and dressed in clean clothes, but there were red marks on his wrists where they had bound him.

Bound him! What he had been through in the last two days, I could not guess. But what confounded me was his fear. He, too, was afraid of me and averted his eyes from my face.

"Gwillim," I whispered. "Kneel down so we can talk." He obeyed and waited. "Gwillim, I take responsibility. I am sorry they put you in prison. It wasn't fair." He said nothing.

"Gwillim, tell me what happened." It was a command, and he obeyed.

"I tried to come after you, but I lost the black pony. So I followed on foot. I could see where you went clearly enough, because the branches were bent and the undergrowth trampled. But of course I could not catch you. After a while I realized that if I followed you, I would never catch up. I figured you would circle back to the clearing. I knew you would be able to speak to him. I knew you would not come off unless—unless something scared you." So that was it. It was his voice that had startled the pony. "When at last I saw you returning, I could not control my joy, Gwen—I mean, my lady, and I shouted."

"I know about that part. Never mind. I'd have done the same. What happened after that? How on earth did you get me back on the pony?"

The ghost of a grin swept his face and was instantly hidden.

"I didn't know what to do. You were bleeding, my lady. There was lots of blood around your head. I thought you were dying. I sat down beside you and cried. And then—" His hushed voice sank so low I had to strain to hear it. "—then *the pony came back to you*. I was sitting there, and he came right out of the forest, right up to you, and nuzzled you. He let me put my belt around his neck. He let me lay you across his back. He let me lead him down the mountain, and he walked so carefully over the stones, you never even slid." There was awe in his voice, and in his face, and I realized with a shock of despair that Gwill had changed.

"The soldiers came and rescued you. They let me put the pony in the paddock before they took me to the king. He is there still. He didn't even try to get away." Suddenly his shyness fled, and he spoke eagerly. "Don't you see, Gwen? It's a sign. After the evil things we thought about by the spring, we were both punished, you immediately and me later on, and then the pony's coming all by himself. It's a sign from the god."

"From which god, Gwill?"

He looked pained. "Does it matter, my lady? It's the proof, you see."

"Proof of what?" My throat ached so it was hard to speak.

"I blasphemed," he said humbly, "and was given a sign. I have no doubts any longer."

"You believe because you saw a sign, but you saw the sign only because you believed."

"Don't," he said quickly. "Please, my lady. Don't say those awful things. You will be punished again."

"I am being punished now," I retorted. "Why do you address me as 'my lady'? I'm 'Gwen' to you, remember?"

He lowered his eyes, and I was instantly sorry I'd said it. I understood, of course. It was the risk I'd had to take to save his honor, but it was a bitter pill to swallow for a proud, brave boy.

"You are the king's daughter," he said slowly, addressing the coverlet. "And I am your servant. A word from your lips saved my mother and sisters from a cruel fate. For this I thank you. Even my father must be obedient to your command and take back what he had put away. The honor of our house is in your hands, my lady."

"Yes, w—well," I stammered, fighting back tears. "I saw no other way. You'd better go."

He rose with dignity, bowed, and turned away. I turned my face to the wall and wept.

2 ✦ GWYNEDD

On my eighth birthday I left my home forever.

My father called me to him one wretched night that winter and, with tears streaming unchecked into his beard, told me that come spring and my eighth birthday, he would send me away. It felt like death. Nothing he said could comfort me. I was not going far away, only into the next kingdom, by the Western Sea, to the house of my mother's sister, whose husband was lord of that land. But in those days, and at that age, it was across the world.

The reason was, he said, that it was the only place I would be safe.

I did not understand at first. He would not tell me that he had felt the first touch of the hand of Death. I thought he meant we should have war.

Wales had been quiet enough. Winter had closed the seas, and the Irish raiders kept to their own coasts. Of the inland fighting to the east and south against Angles and Saxons, news filtered in from time to time. But the names of the strange places and kings, of Cornwall, Strathclyde, Rheged, Lothian, of Cador, Ector, Urien, and Lot—these were foreign words, foreign lands, foreign princes. For the Kingdom of Northgallis was my country and Wales the limit of the civilized world.

When my father fell ill that winter, he called his sons to him. To the eldest, Gwarthgydd, he bequeathed the major part of his kingdom and the king's house at Cameliard. To the others he gave lands of their own to keep independently, provided, and he made this condition clear, that they follow and fight for the High King Uther Pendragon against his enemies.

For the king my father believed very strongly that the safety and, indeed, the future of Wales depended on the High King's desperate efforts to contain the Saxon invasions on eastern coasts.

And he knew whereof he spoke. He had been a young man when the High King Vortigern had invited the Saxons to Britain's shores to help him quell the rebellious Picts who threatened from the north. These Picts, a fierce and primitive race of thieves and bandits, had badgered the country incessantly and for generations, since the last Roman legions had left the land. But the Saxons were worse. At least the Picts had no organization and never stayed in the land they conquered, but retreated to their own homes to sing their victory paeans. The Saxons stayed. Vortigern found that, once he had invited them in, he could not make them leave and was forced to reward them with land in return for their service against the Picts. He gave them small plots along the southeastern shores and thought, the shortsighted fool, that that should content them. But within five years their families and all their relations had come to join them, and the Saxon colonies grew.

As everyone knows, their numbers increased until their lands could not hold them, and their war leaders Hengist and Horsa were a greater threat to King Vortigern than ever the Picts had been. Vortigern even married a Saxon queen, Hengist's daughter. After that no true Celt would follow him, and he lost his power to the Saxon horde. It was Ambrosius who saved us. Aurelius Ambrosius, brother of the rightful king whom Vortigern had murdered, invaded from Less Britain with an army of twenty thousand and fought Vortigern to a bloody victory. My father fought in that battle, where the old wolf and his Saxon queen were smoked out of their hill fort and burned alive. And he fought in the battle at Caer Konan, where Hengist was beaten, when Merlin himself appeared out of thin air to predict Ambrosius' victory. Had it not been for Ambrosius, we should all have been as degenerate as the Picts.

The great Ambrosius, and his younger brother Uther, gathered the many British kings together, from Lothian and Rheged to Dyfed and Dumnonia, and bound them with oaths of loyalty to the High King of Britain. Fighting together under a strong war leader was our only hope of stemming the Saxon tide, so my father was wont to exhort his warriors on cold winter nights, when war looked distant and glorious. But this my father deeply believed, even when he was called upon to take arms and fight in Uther's army. And he saw to it that his sons should follow his example.

Now, after fifteen years of vigilance and fighting constant small battles to hold the kingdoms together and give the people peace,

Uther was getting old. I thought my father foresaw war coming closer to home and was sending me temporarily to the coastal kingdom of Gwynedd to live under the care of King Pellinore and Queen Alyse, until Northgallis should be safe for me once more.

It was a sad leave-taking. I adored my father. He had not held my mother's death against me, and I think he loved me more tenderly because I reminded him of her. He was a good king and a strong one, but he never used his sword unnecessarily, nor took joy in killing. The worst I can say of him is that he spoiled me and knew it. I worshipped him.

"My little Gwen," he said, hugging me tightly as the escort made ready to leave early on the first of May. "I will come visit you at summer's end, the gods willing. You must make a place for yourself in your mother's family. You have a cousin for company, and they will give you book learning, which I cannot do here. You should know more than I do, my dear, if the witch is to be believed. King Pellinore is a wise man and has a scholar in his house. There are fine horses there, too, my sweet. You will not be without your favorite entertainment. Now dry those pretty eyes and be a brave princess. And always remember," he said under his breath, "always remember who you are and what you will be."

I was used to his references to the hag's prophecy and nodded obediently. Ever since the fortelling at my birth I was held to be a wonder by the Welsh. On more than one occasion I heard fantastic stories told about me that bore no relation to the truth, but that the people willingly believed. Thanks to Giselda, they expected me to bring them honor. This is a hard thing to live with, even now.

Thus I left Northgallis, but I never saw his dear face again, for he died when summer came and was buried before the news reached me.

My cousin Elaine was a gossip, even at seven. She befriended me on sight and made me feel at home from my first moment. She was eager to have a companion near her own age to talk to and play with, as her mother and the nurses were busy with three younger sons. I loved her for this. She was gay and warm-hearted, bold where I was shy, open and loving where I was reserved. I have never forgotten her sweetness to me at that time when it mattered most. For remembrance of this, I have struggled to forgive her cruel betrayal, for without her love and friendship in my childhood, I should not have had the courage to face what the fates have brought me.

While Ailsa unpacked my trunk and scant belongings in Elaine's room, Elaine took my arm and gave me a tour of her home. She showed me everything, from basement scullery to the turrets on the western tower, where the sentries kept watch all year for Irish pirates. She never stopped talking. She knew everything: reports of Saxon fighting to the east; which queens were witches, and which kings coveted another's land; who in the village was engaged to whom, and which of the kitchen slaves had given birth to an illegitimate child. I laughed to hear her tales, told with a gleam in her sky-blue eyes and a light in her happy face. Indeed, within an hour of my arrival, it was possible to forget, at least for a while, the hard two days' journey and my dear father's parting kiss.

When she took me to the sentry tower I had my first sight of the sea. It seemed to stretch on forever, away in the distance, low and gray and empty and immensely sad. Elaine was delighted at my amazement.

"Have you never seen the sea, then? Why, we ride upon the shore on holidays, or when Iakos gives us the day free. I have even been upon it, in a golden ship with silver sails! Well, it was pretty fancy, anyhow. My father sailed to Caer Narvon last September, and he let me come aboard before they departed. It was wonderful—the very floor I stood upon rolled this way and that, like a cradle, almost! I should love to have an adventure at sea!"

I smiled at her. "I would be afraid to feel the floor beneath me move so," I said. "But I should love to ride along the shore."

"Oh, yes! I have heard how you love horses. Let's go down to the stable, and I'll show you my pony. That is"—with a doubtful look at me—"if you're not too tired. Grannic says I mustn't tire you. She says we must take special care of you. Are you sickly, or something?"

"No, of course not. I think she means because I am your mother's sister's daughter, and kin to you. That's all."

But Elaine still looked uncertain. "But you're different from other people, aren't you?"

I seemed to feel a cold hand upon my neck. "Whatever do you mean?"

"Oh, now you're mad, Gwen. I'm really sorry. It's just something I overheard once. Nobody told me anything. I don't know anything about it."

"What did you overhear?"

"Promise that you won't be angry with me?"

"Elaine, I will not be angry with you. I promise."

"Well, didn't a witch put a spell on you at birth?" I gasped, but she went on. "Not a bad spell, a good spell. Aren't you going to marry a great king and rule over all of us someday?"

A cold shiver ran through me. I found myself furious that the prophecy had followed me even here. I wondered in sudden despair if there was anyone in all of wide Wales who had not heard it.

"I shall do no such thing, silly girl. My father is one among many kings. His lands are less wide than King Pellinore's. You believe in old wives' tales, and you a Christian? I thought your God frowned on magic."

Elaine was undaunted. "But *everybody* knows there are witches. And wizards, as well. Have you never heard of Merlin the Enchanter? He can see the future in a raindrop and vanish into thin air! All the world knows this."

"And many people who have no such power pass themselves off as witches with skill and luck. I am not different, Elaine. As my father is a king, no doubt in time he will marry me off to the finest Welsh lord he can find, but the rest is nonsense. Truly it is. Rule the land, indeed! I shall never rule over you, Elaine. Of that I am quite sure."

She grinned in relief. "Good, because I like being first." If I gave her ease, I am glad, but I was frightened. It was the first time I had voiced my own beliefs about the prophecy, and I was stunned to find how vehemently I resented old Giselda's interference. I was more unhappy to learn that people here knew and believed her words. It occurred to me for the first time, as I stood on the turret beside Elaine, looking out at the strange sea, that I might live under that cloud my whole life. I had insisted I was not different. But if everyone thought that I was, did that not make me so?

In the stables I forgot my fears. King Pellinore had many fine animals, all the sturdy mountain horses that breed freely in the hills of Wales. And Elaine had a pretty fat pony with a fine, dry face and great, dark eyes.

"His name is Petros. It means 'rock.' Iakos says it is a good name for a princess' pony. He's very lazy and does not like to move. This makes him safe to ride!" She laughed gaily at her jest and let me pat his warm neck and stroke the glossy coat. "Mother says you know how to ride already. Did you have your own pony in Northgallis?"

"Yes, a lovely white one. I found him running wild in the hills, and he let me ride him."

Elaine looked put out. "Did you bring him with you?"

"No, I—before I left, I let him go back into the hills. He belonged there."

She brightened again. "Well, Mother said you may take your pick of the next batch they bring in, as long as he gets along with Petros. That's a rare honor, you know. It's because she heard you were skilled."

I felt my face flush with pleasure. Perhaps having oneself talked about wasn't such a bad thing, after all. "I must thank her for the offer. And who is Iakos?"

"Iakos is my tutor—I mean *our* tutor. He is teaching me Latin and writing and figures, although not too much of that because I hate it. Also music. Leonora, the queen's woman, will teach us stitchery and weaving, and also housekeeping when we are older. There's a lot to learn to be a good queen, isn't there?"

She cocked her head sideways and looked up at me shrewdly. She seemed to me to be ready for anything, full of confidence and life, willing to try whatever came to her hand. I envied her enormously. I was completely untutored in any feminine skills. My childhood had been spent with my doting father and my rough, grown half-brothers. I could run, ride, shoot with bow and arrow, and hawk as well as any youth my age. For my fifth birthday Gwarth had given me a young falcon, fallen from his nest and saved just in time, to raise for my own. He had helped me to train it, and I learned to fashion jesses from worked leather and had made my own glove. But I instinctively kept these accomplishments a secret from Elaine, who I feared might despise them. Of embroidery and the weaving of war cloaks, tasks every woman of even moderate birth must learn in order to marry, I knew nothing.

And of her religion, the worship of the Christian God, I knew very little. But there was a priest among the household staff, and I knew I would be instructed in the new ways. This had been my father's only reservation in sending me to my mother's people. They had been Christians for two generations, ever since an Irish martyr landed upon their coast and with wit and charm persuaded them to turn their backs on the Elder spirits. Whether my father had thought it an inevitable consequence of his plans for me, or whether he recognized that the tide of change was sweeping the land, he had consented to my instruction. So I was brought into the fold of the jealous Christian God, my feet were set upon the True Path, and the little deities of hill and stream, rock and high place, were left behind.

* * *

It was a busy summer. Elaine's mother, Queen Alyse, kept us to our tasks and allowed us little time for mischief-making. As I was to find, her word was law. To her credit, she believed her daughter deserving of the same education she gave her sons and made no excuses to Iakos on our behalf. I tried my best to please her in everything, but it was not easy to accomplish. She was not unkind, but neither was she warm. Tall and beautifully featured, with the family's fairness and a majestic bearing, she did not welcome confidences from children. Even Pellinore was half afraid to cross her.

At our first meeting she looked me over carefully, placing her hand on my chin and turning my face toward the light.

"So you are Elen's daughter," she said thoughtfully, after I had made my speech of thanks for taking me in. "I pray you will be as well behaved. We will teach you manners here, Guinevere, and make a princess of you." I was tempted to retort that I was a princess already and that my father had taught me manners, but I held my tongue, afraid that to speak would give the lie to my assertion. "You would do well," she said coolly, "to follow Elaine in everything." It was advice I learned to take.

That summer the old High King, Uther Pendragon, who had held the kingdoms of Britain together for nearly fifteen years, began to fail. Messengers rode into the castle every week with news. It was said he could no longer sit a horse, but had to be carried to battle in a litter, like a woman. Some of the men scoffed at the rumor, denying that any soldier of mettle would follow an invalid war leader. Indeed, it was a shocking thought. But King Pellinore himself believed it, saying that Uther was the best warrior in the kingdoms, afoot, astride, or abed, and only a fool would be too proud to follow him. So the dissenters kept their grumbling quiet, sharpened their spears, polished their swords, and waited.

The Saxons were massing, they said, clogging the shores in the southeast, and Colgrin their leader was making alliances with the petty kings there, gathering strength for an attack on the High King. But weeks wore on, and no royal messenger came to summon King Pellinore and his men. What came instead were the rains. We had had drought all winter, and now, after a warm, dry spring, the skies opened over all Wales and drowned the fertile valleys. Crops rotted where they stood, the rich soil was scoured from the land by raging rivers, and sheep and horse foundered in the mired pastures. Ailsa muttered charms under her breath against evil spirits; the miller's boy went mad and threw himself in the sea; the queen's garden was spoiled, and the cooks complained bitterly; even the priest was seen to cross himself whenever the clouds grew black.

Every day brought news of some sort: local news of local catastrophes; distant news of discontent, uprisings, invasions, and assaults. A blight lay upon the land. Some said God was displeased that ignorant souls persisted in the worship of Mithra and would give no victories to pagan soldiers. But Elaine and I scoffed at that. Colgrin and his Saxons worshipped gods far more barbarous than Mithra! Some said the land was failing as the High King failed and that we would not recover until we had a new King. This argument was no longer whispered in corners between nervous warriors; it was spoken aloud at the king's supper table, after the women had left. Elaine and I heard it ourselves.

Of course, we were not in the hall. We were eavesdropping. Elaine showed me this secret in my first week there. Along the parapet between the east and south turrets was a smallish crack in the stone, and through this crack we could peer down into the smoky hall. This fissure was protected by the guardhouse wall from the east wind, else it would have been discovered when the rain blew in. But if we covered ourselves in our dark, hooded cloaks and crept up past the guardhouse when the sentries were warming themselves by the fire, or standing at their posts at either turret, we could crouch unseen by the crack and learn of the high matters young maids were never allowed to know.

To do the guards justice, they were good men and loyal to the king, but it never occurred to them that the young princesses were not abed past dark, or would be curious about what rough soldiers said in the drinking hall. But we were always curious and never afraid to listen when we knew a courier had come. Only the very worst weather could keep us away. Ailsa and Grannic, Elaine's nurse, slept outside our door, it is true. But they were loud snorers and deep sleepers, embarrassingly easy to deceive.

Thus we learned of the country's discontent, and the threat of war that loomed on the horizon, a war that would change our lives, whatever the outcome. All of King Pellinore's men were loyal to the Pendragon banner, and trained almost daily in the courtyard. But as the summer wore on and the crops and animals died, and men went mad from hunger and lack of sun, they were called to their lands to put down unrest among the farmers and oversee the care of their own families, so that the king's fighting force was scattered. There were barely enough men at court to get up a hunt, and no one cared to hawk when the gloom lay so heavy on the land. Talk at dinner invariably returned to one theme: would not the High King at last recall his only son Arthur from his secret fastness and reveal him to the lords and set him to lead us against the Saxons?

Everyone in Britain knew this tale. I had been raised on it. Indeed, it was the one tale, in my father's country, which was better known than mine. When Uther Pendragon was crowned High King of Britain, he had fallen desperately in love with Ygraine, wife of Gorolis, Duke of Cornwall. She was only twenty, and Gorolis a grizzled warrior of fifty. Some said Merlin the Enchanter had put a spell on the King at his coronation feast, so that as soon as he saw her, he had no peace of mind, but planned how he could take her and yet not wreck the Kingdom by so doing. Remembering stories of my dear father's infatuation for my mother, I did not think that sudden love needed any supernatural explanation, but I believed with the rest of the world, that the famous enchanter had been responsible for the clever plan that brought Uther his heart's desire. Gorolis removed his wife from the High King's reach as soon as etiquette permitted and brought her to the impregnable fortress of Tintagel on the Cornwall coast. He and his fighting men repaired to a fine fighting fortress that guarded the route, in case the High King should follow. As soon as the official feasting was over, Uther, and Merlin with him, came with a large army and camped just out of bowshot. It looked like the fragile kingdom would soon be split by war. But Merlin changed the King by magic arts into the very likeness of Gorolis, and thus disguised, he rode along the track to Tintagel and was admitted by the guard, all unknowing. Men believe that the young duchess was also deceived, but no woman I know believes this. It is a known fact that Ygraine was a faithful and loving wife to King Uther, obedient to his every wish to the end of their days, as if the flame of love never died in her heart. I will leave it there. During the night they were together, when Arthur was conceived, Gorolis led his troops in a surprise attack against the High King's army, which is treason, and the old duke was killed in the fighting. Uther married Ygraine as soon as he decently could, before her pregnancy began to show. But out of guilt for the death of Gorolis, he refused to acknowledge the son that was born, and three nights after his birth handed him to Merlin to safeguard and raise. Since then the boy had been in Merlin's keeping, but no one knew where. Some said even Uther did not know.

King Uther and Queen Ygraine had no other sons in all the years of their marriage. And now, with Uther ill and the Saxon power growing in the east, men said it was time for the Prince to be brought forth and for Uther to acknowledge him. Wales would rise for him, that was clear. But there were lands in the east, already menaced by the Saxons, that were less certain. King Lot of Lothian had met with Colgrin, and no one knew if he would support Uther when the time came or try to supplant him. Ambrosius' fragile kingdom might be split forever, if Prince Arthur did not soon appear.

Elaine and I were careful never to let slip any comment that would reveal how much we knew about events. But when news came, at midsummer, of my father's death, and Queen Alyse gave me a new pony of my own as a comfort gift, Elaine and I would ride along the shore, ahead of the escort, and have long conferences. Elaine could talk of little else but Arthur. No one had seen him, no one really knew if he even existed, but Elaine knew all about him. She even knew what he looked like.

"He's dark," she confided. "Black hair and blue eyes, the true Celt. And stronger than any man his age."

"Which is all of thirteen," I pointed out, grinning. We were five and six years younger, but girls could be married off at twelve, while boys had to wait until fifteen to be made warriors. Elaine was undaunted.

"He's a Christian, too, so the men will follow him."

"How can he be Christian if Merlin the Enchanter has raised him? Everyone knows Merlin is a pagan and a powerful one. It is said he speaks to the gods directly and has seen Mithra himself slaying the Bull."

Elaine crossed herself quickly, then made a sign against the ancient evil spirits that was not Christian at all. "Hush, Gwen, don't say such things! You're blaspheming, I know it! Have you no fear? Anyway, Queen Ygraine is a Christian, even if the High King is not, and she wouldn't have him raised by a pagan household. And how can he lead Christian soldiers if he isn't one himself?"

"King Uther does. I don't think soldiers care so much, as long as their leader is successful. And I don't know about Queen Ygraine. I mean, she can't be much of a mother if she was content to give her firstborn son away three days after she bore him. She may not care how he is raised." I saw I had hurt Elaine, who adored her image of Prince Arthur, and I was ashamed of myself. "Never mind, Elaine. You are probably right. I'm sure he's a devout Christian like Father Martin and handsome, as well. He can probably do everything." But as her humor was restored, I fell to teasing her again. "But perhaps he is fair. King Uther was red-headed in his youth, they say, although now he is gray."

Elaine was unmovable on this point. "You forget his descent. Uther's line is dark. Uther's brother Ambrosius was dark, and Constantius, their father, was dark, and so on back to the Emperor Maximus, founder of the line."

"Who was Iberian, and not Celt," I reminded her. "And black-eyed, to boot."

Elaine sniffed. "Dark hair can be Celt, too, and blue eyes certainly are. Maximus married a Welsh princess from our own country, Princess Elen, and she had blue eyes. She's famous for it. Dark, brilliant blue, like the sea in a summer storm. She's my kin." Then she stopped, remembering that she was related to the famous Elen through her mother's line, and therefore I was descended from her, too. She looked at me cautiously. I knew already what she saw, because the color of my eyes had been compared to the Princess Elen's all my life.

"Well," I said quickly, "it's no wonder we think so much of Prince Arthur, since we are both kin to him, if you go far enough back."

Elaine looked delighted. This was the kindest thing I had ever yet said about Arthur, and she took it as a victory. The truth was, I disparaged him only to tease Elaine; but the skeptical attitude, once adopted, stuck. From that summer on, I was always finding fault with him, if only because Elaine thought him so perfect.

The sun returned when September came, but it was too late. The smell of rotting growth and mud stank in the river valleys, and men and beasts died from mysterious fevers. Water lay everywhere on the ground, breeding insects and disease. We could not bury our dead for the mud, and burned them instead on funeral pyres like the dead of the Saxon savages. The queen kept us to the castle and forbade our rides upon the shore, fearing we would catch noxious vapors and fall ill. Indeed, the youngest of Elaine's brothers fell to the fever in September, and the queen was prostrate with grief. Men muttered under their breaths of omens and witchcraft; women wore charms against ancient evils, the Christian women secretly and others, like Ailsa, actually jingled and clicked as they walked from the jumble of talismans they carried. Small offerings were made daily at the wayside shrines. The village folk had not forgotten the Elders. King Pellinore, saddened and restless, called in his men from their homes and drilled them mercilessly in preparation for action, any action, to keep their minds from dwelling on the death and stagnation that enveloped Britain.

And then finally, toward the end of that interminable month, the royal courier arrived. Elaine and I were on the eastern wall when he rode up the valley on his tired horse, spattered with mud and so exhausted he could barely stay in his saddle. We knew who he was by the leather pouch at his belt, and we exchanged glances behind the sentry's back, knowing we would creep out that night to overhear the king's conference.

The news was thrilling indeed. King Uther Pendragon was gathering his forces at Caer Eden, a week's march north, and all loyal Britons were called to arm and join him there to meet the Saxon attack. The time had come. Cheering filled the hall. The men sounded wild with happiness, as if the courier were bringing them tidings of great joy. The king proposed a toast, and as the men turned to their tankards and the noise died down, we heard Arthur's name.

"Will Arthur be there?" "Yes, will the great Enchanter reveal him now?" "Will Uther acknowledge him, I wonder, and give him a command?" "He's just a boy—how could he?" "Ah, but he's the royal heir, with black magic behind him, and we'll follow him anywhere."

King Pellinore hushed them, looking fierce under his bushy black eyebrows, but the courier fidgeted nervously. He was not charged with any official message about the prince, but rumor had it—rumor, mind you—that Merlin had been sent for. And where Merlin was . . .

This was the best news to come to Wales in years, and within two days every able-bodied fighting man had marched north to fight the Saxons, confident in the certain victory that the fabled Arthur would bring. Elaine was beside herself with excitement, but I felt the loss of the men keenly. There was no more news, no more eavesdropping, no more feeling a part of events. We had shrunk to a household of women, and our chief occupations were putting the castle to rights, getting in what little harvest there was, weaving and sewing against the inevitable winter cold, and for me and Elaine, uninterrupted lessons with Father Martin and Iakos.

We did not hear about the battle for two whole months, when it was long over and the glory of the battlefield had faded in the minds of the wounded and maimed, who were the first to come home.

3 🌸 KING ARTHUR

Queen Alyse organized a primitive hospital in the castle out-buildings. It was not primitive by the standards of the day, only by comparison to what I have seen since, for there were no learned men of healing in Gwynedd, no army physicians, no Merlin. We were a community of women with skill to heal minor wounds such as men get hunting. Those soldiers who made it back to us were grateful for our attentions, but they were halfway to recovery before ever setting foot in the sickrooms. The worst wounded had died in the field hospital at Caer Eden, and more on the road home.

Elaine and I were not allowed to treat the men directly on account of our youth, and I was grateful for this. Nursing repelled me; I had not the stomach for maimed limbs and open sores and the stench of sickness. We were happy to help the washing women hang the clean linens to dry and fold them away, sweet-smelling and herb-scented, until the nurses needed them. We helped to change the bedding on the palettes that lined the floor and were allowed to bring around cool water for the men to drink.

One day, as Elaine and I stood outside the sickrooms, folding linens, I began to hum, and then sing, an old Welsh song I had learned in Northgallis about the beauty of Wales, her fertile meadows where sheep grazed in summer, her shining ponds and white-frothed streams, her cool forests full of game, and the crown of her glory, glittering Snow Mountain, where the gods walked among the clouds. Elaine loved the song and begged me to teach it to her, so I repeated it for her sake. Then we brought our folded linens to Cissa, the queen's lady-in-waiting who was in charge of the washing. To my amazement, she curtsied low before me.

"The queen's compliments, Lady Guinevere," she said softly, "and would you be pleased to continue singing, for the men were

29

quiet and restful just now, and seemed relieved of pain. The queen tells me they had tears in their eyes, and indeed, my lady, it was beautiful to hear."

I stared, astonished that the queen favored me with such attention, and assured Cissa I would be delighted to sing. From that day forward, singing to the men was my chief duty, and Queen Alyse had a cushioned chair brought for me and set just inside the door, so that all could hear the song, and yet I was not overcome by the sickroom vapors. To show their gratitude, the men began to call me the Lark of Gwynedd.

As men healed and were allowed to sit outside in the afternoon sun and take exercise on the grounds, Elaine and I learned from them all we wanted to know about the great things that had happened in the north. To be sure, King Pellinore had sent his queen a messenger bearing news of the glorious victory over Colgrin and his Saxon hordes, of Uther's death and of young Arthur's succession. With the kings of Britain united behind him, the new King pursued the Saxons eastward, and Pellinore went with him, leaving Gwynedd in the capable hands of Queen Alyse.

But these were dry facts, and we sought among the convalescing soldiers for those who could tell us what we really wanted to know. Finally we found Corwin, a twenty-year-old foot soldier who had suffered a broken leg. He was lucky that the bones had not pierced the skin. Merlin himself, he said, had splinted the leg and prophesied that it would knit cleanly and straight. He had since fashioned himself a pair of crutches and got about easily enough. He had a ready tongue, a bard's gift for exaggeration, and a lazy nature. He spun us tales by the hour, and we believed them all.

"Tell us about the battle!" Elaine cried, settling down at his feet, her face aglow. "Did Prince Arthur fight?"

"Did he indeed!" Corwin exclaimed, grinning. "Why, he won it for us, you may be sure, and proclaimed himself by the deed, even if he was the last to know it."

"What do you mean, the last to know it?"

Corwin laughed. "Why, just what I said, my lady. When he came to Caer Eden with Sir Ector of Galava, he was more a body servant to Ector's son Kay than a warrior. By rights, he's a year or two short of making a soldier. He'd no more idea of who he was than Kay did himself, or I, or any man there, excepting only Ector, King Uther and that sly fox Merlin. And as far as anyone could see, Merlin was there alone, standing silently with his arms folded into his sleeves and a face as dark as stormclouds, watching everything, saying nothing, keeping his own counsel. No one gave a second glance to Ector's fosterling."

"Ector's fosterling?" I wondered.

"Oh, never mind that now!" Elaine cut in. "Go on, Corwin, tell us about the battle!"

Corwin settled himself among the cushions we had brought him. He had a Welshman's love of a good tale, and this had all the earmarks of an afternoon's work. "It was midmorning when we saw them coming across the river plain. You should have seen them—thousands of Saxons—blond giants with paint on their faces and four-foot moustaches, whirling their two-headed axes over their heads in a mad frenzy of noise. Wild men, they were, screaming uncouth paeans—I don't mind admitting it to you girls, but my bones were shaking."

Elaine giggled. "You're no soldier, then. Soldiers are never afraid."

"Aren't they, my lady? Well, that's as may be. I can only speak for myself. And yet I'll wager there wasn't a man on the field who saw them coming who didn't wish he were safely home in bed."

Elaine was scandalized. "You call Prince Arthur a coward? And King Uther? And Pellinore, my father?"

Corwin shook his head quickly. "Certainly not, little princess. Brave men, all of them. But if a man has no fear to face and overcome, where is bravery? He is a fool, that's all."

"Oh, stuff and nonsense. You're just making excuses. Go on with the battle!"

"He was, until you interrupted," I pointed out, and was rewarded with a bold retort and an angry shake of her head.

"I'll tell you this," Corwin cut in. "They almost took us. We were all looking about for Prince Arthur when the trumpets sounded, but no one saw him anywhere. Half the men watched Uther, half watched Merlin. But Uther lay abed upon his litter, with his own guards in attendance, and Merlin busied himself in the field hospital, paying no attention to anyone. Men began to doubt the prince had come. When the Saxons attacked, we gave up hope and followed the High King's litter onto the field."

Corwin's voice fell into the singsong lilt of the storyteller, and we hugged our knees and listened, enraptured.

"The Saxons attacked at the center of the line, where the High King's litter was. So savage they were, we could not hold them, and fell back against the onslaught. They pressed hard, eager to get to Uther, a sick king, and have it over early. Now, Sir Ector of Galava led the right flank, and saw his chance to cut the Saxons off. Good soldier that he is! If Lot, who led the left, had had the sense to do the same, the villainous dogs would have been swallowed up and surrounded. But Lot stood his ground and looked the other way."

"I hope he was hanged for his treachery!" Elaine exclaimed hotly.

Corwin laughed. "On the contrary, brave lass, he rides at the side of the young King as they chase Colgrin toward the sea."

Elaine objected violently, but I said, "Since he is alive, it is the best place for him, where Arthur can keep an eye on him."

Corwin regarded me thoughtfully. "So many have said, my lady, and Merlin one of them, if rumors be true."

"Well, I'd have killed him myself if I were king!" Elaine cried emphatically. "But go on, Corwin, what happened next? Don't take all day."

"For God's sake, Elaine—" I began, but Corwin raised a hand.

"Bide a bit, young ladies, and let me tell the tale. You will know it all, in time. Well, there we were, face to face with the stinking Saxon hordes. Had Lothian grown roots in the hill, that he could not move? Was he waiting, as some were saying, to see which way the battle went? If the Saxons got to the King, he could join them from the flank and cut *us* off—the lines wavered, uncertain. Good Ector led the charge from the right and drove deep, with his son Kay right at his side. But an ax got his leg and he lost his sword; he had to withdraw. Young Kay tried to take his place—he fought hard, he's a valiant soldier—but he had no sense of the battlefield, of the flow of things, of where he was. He was pushing too hard in the wrong place, and the seasoned warriors all knew it. The charge began to waver, the lines began to weave, the Saxons scented the kill; for a moment it seemed that all was lost—the charge, the Briton positions, the field, the day, the High King, the Kingdom. For a moment—the same moment—every man on the field knew it, wherever he was. It was one of those moments when time stops, when the balance between two futures—defeat and victory, death and life, evil and good fortune—lies on a thin edge of chance." Corwin paused. We could have heard a leaf fall in the silence. "But it was no chance the unknown boy rode forward, raised his sword, gave the orders in a voice that brooked no hesitation, and saved the day. Out of nowhere he came; but he knew what to do, and every man there followed him. I followed him myself, and I don't know why. I'd never seen him before. But he'd a cool head on his shoulders, and he fought a damned smart fight. Before old Colgrin knew what had happened, he found himself pushed hard against the hill where Lothian waited, and King Lot, forced to choose and seeing a new commander bidding fair to take his place at the King's right hand, cast his future with the British and attacked. That was the end of it, really. It was all over but the mopping up."

"And then?" Elaine asked excitedly. "Surely everyone knew by then? Surely King Uther proclaimed him?"

"No, my lady. It's a busy time, after battle, with the field to clear and the wounded to tend. We all found our own camps and took stock of who was left."

"But you must have wondered who he was," I said, "and where he had come from."

"Oh, he was the talk of the army, of course. Who was the new commander? No one knew his name or had seen his badge. The word went round he was a child, a dogsbody, a nameless lad who tagged along in Kay of Galava's wake. Ector's fosterling, they said, meaning Ector's bastard, born on the wrong side of the blanket and good only for errands and hard labor."

"No! How did they dare!"

"Who was to know? A few bright souls wondered if it might be Prince Arthur in disguise—such a disguise!—but no one knew, and no one liked to wager on such a long shot. All that long night we carried the dead from the field, dug the grave pits, sorted their belongings, and tended to our wounds. That's when I broke my leg, in a scuffle with a half-dead Saxon who attacked me when I took his armband. In the field hospital I saw my cousin Durwen—the bardling, we called him, because he wanted to be a bard, he had a gift for it. He was delirious with pain from a slice across his thigh, but he had already made a song about the battle. "The Wrath of the Nameless Prince" he called it. He had sung it for Merlin, he claimed, as he stitched his leg, and Merlin had smiled."

Elaine wrinkled her nose. "Ector's fosterling? No, Corwin, it's too ignoble. Tell us rather that Merlin raised him in the Magic Isles across the Western Sea and brought him forth just in time to save us from the Saxons!"

"I'm telling you what happened, if you'll be polite like your cousin and wait for me to get there." Corwin winked at me and took another pull from his flask. "When the work was done, the men who were well and whole caroused till dawn. There were plenty of girls in Caer Eden to toast our victory. Ah, those lovely northern lasses—" He stopped, recollecting where he was, and cleared his throat. "Beg pardon. But I cursed the misfortune of my leg, I can tell you that. At daybreak we gave thanks to Mithra in a formal ceremony, with King Uther in attendance, pale as a nether spirit. And that night there was to be a formal victory feast. Rumor had it he was going to bring forth the prince at last and name his heir—he was dying on his feet, anyone could see it. Men looked all about for Prince Arthur but could not find him. Meanwhile, Ector's fosterling was in the hospital with Merlin, visiting the wounded and offering his arm to Ector so the man could walk. By daylight you could see he was only a beardless boy, and hopes fell." Corwin paused. "These things I saw and can swear to. The rest I know only because the camp was alive with rumors, and I spoke with men who had been at the victory feast, and—and at what came after."

Elaine and I looked at each other. He was making the sign against enchantment behind his back, and we wondered why. We had certainly heard no rumors of magic from the men, only bragging about the battle itself.

"Then suddenly, toward sunset, talk began to go through camp the King was dying. Everyone fell still. The guard was doubled around Uther's tent, and all the lords gathered inside, including Ector with Kay and the fosterling, and Merlin, and the kings of Rheged, Strathclyde, Cornwall, Elmet, Lothian, and Gwynedd. I can't tell you just what happened, because I wasn't there, but word went round that Uther, on his deathbed, proclaimed the fosterling to be his own son by the queen Ygraine, named him his heir, and bade the kings, follow him. The lords took it as well as they might: Ector pleased as punch; Cornwall, Rheged, Strathclyde, and our own good King Pellinore cheered the lad and swore him faith. But Lothian was furious. Lot had schemed for years to become High King, betrothing Uther's bastard daughter for the purpose. She was there, you know, the beautiful Morgause, to persuade her father to the choice. But they reckoned without Arthur, those two." He turned to spit, then recollected his audience and contented himself with a gruff rumble in his throat. "There might have been a brawl, except that in the middle of the fracas, Uther died. And that put an end to the celebrations." The sadness in Corwin's face bespoke his loyalty to Uther. I was moved to see it. "It's an uncommon bad omen, victory or no victory, the High King dying while the Saxons still lay encamped across the river. Why, the smoke from their funeral pyres kept us up coughing half the night. A new King had to be chosen, and fast. And while young Arthur had been proclaimed, no one felt easy about making a child a King with such a deadly enemy so near. In the interim, King Lot took charge."

"Traitor!" Elaine cried.

"No, my lady, not really. It needed the strong hand of an experienced warrior the soldiers trusted. It was best for everyone. And who else to turn to? Merlin might have stepped forward, but he did not. He returned to the field hospital, and young Arthur with him, looking dazed and grim. Lot announced we would hold the victory feast as planned, in Uther's honor, and that afterward a council of commanders could discuss the wisdom of Uther's recommendation and choose the next High King."

"Uther's recommendation!" Elaine bristled. "How dare he! It is treason!"

"Nonsense," I retorted, tired of her interruptions. "We are not Roman yet. Kings are still chosen by the lords who must serve them."

"If the king's son or his nephew are not worthy!" Elaine cried, beside herself. "But *Arthur* is the King's son! He *is* worthy! Were they blind? Hadn't he just won the battle for them?"

"Yes," I replied calmly, "it is easy enough to sit here safe in Wales and say so, but imagine being a soldier in the field. What Corwin says makes sense to me. They were all grown men, kings and lords and warriors; they did not want to serve a boy."

"Exactly so, my lady," Corwin said sadly. "It is ever the way of men not to see what is before their noses."

"What happened at the victory feast?" I asked.

Corwin frowned. "Well, they fell to arguing as soon as the wine went round. I have this from Durwen, who dragged himself from bed to accompany Pellinore. There were lords in the hall who were in league with Lothian and objected that a boy not yet fourteen was too young to lead a troop of seasoned warriors, much less a kingdom. Some argued long and loud on Lot's behalf: Cyndeg of Gore, the snake Aguisel, a few others. Lot himself said nothing. Be sure he had paid them well beforehand for their speeches. They said the High King's dying in the face of Saxons was an omen, and that Britain itself would die if we did not change the line."

"Had they already forgotten who brought them victory? What better omen could there be than that?" Elaine was shouting.

"Soldiers are superstitious," Corwin replied, "as you very well know. Black Celts from the hills of Wales are the worst of all. There was many a man in that hall who took it as a sign from the gods that Uther's line ended with Uther's death. There were cries of 'Lothian! Lot for High King!' from one side of the hall, and cries of 'Arthur!' from the other. And then, when the hall was near to erupting into open warfare, Merlin the Enchanter arose before the crowd. One look from him froze the wagging tongues, and when it was quiet, he spoke. It did not matter, he told them, what choice men made. This King had been ordained by gods a hundred years before his birth. He was the Light of Britain; his time had come. That day he had proved his prowess before them all. He was Chosen, and the gods that made men would prove it so, that very night. Lot stood up and objected—he has more courage than I have, to face Merlin in the midst of a pronouncement, I grant him that—Lot stood up and objected that an army of men needed a man to lead them, not a boy, and talk about gods and magic and foretelling was so much stuff and nonsense, to borrow my lady's phrase. Merlin, cool as ice, gestured toward the unarmed boy, and said that Arthur stood before them without a sword, for a reason. It was not Uther's sword that would bring him into Kingship, but one given by the gods themselves. That very night, in the presence of them all, they would give the Sword into his hand, the Sword that would protect Britain from her enemies for as long as Arthur held it." Corwin paused. "Now, Merlin, besides having power from the gods, besides being wise beyond the wisdom of men, Merlin is also a showman of the first class. He let the questions run through the hall like wind through a hayfield, and then he let the murmuring die down, until all was still. And then, when he commanded every eye and every ear, he told the history of the Sword. It was, he said, the Sword of the Emperor Maximus."

Elaine and I gasped. All Welsh children were brought up on the story of Macsen Wledig, as the Welsh called Maximus, but the tale of the Sword was new to us. Magnus Maximus had been the last Roman commander in Britain; when the Romans pulled out, Macsen stayed with his Welsh princess Elen and forged the hill tribes of Britain into a Kingdom. It was the Sword of Maximus that turned aside the Saxons, the Picts, and the Irish in the dark time men call the Flood Year. Romano-British civilization teetered on the edge of extinction then, but Maximus' disciplined troops beat back the savages and won for Britain a breathing space of peace. He was acclaimed Emperor of Britain by the people and kept the peace in the Roman way.

But at length his ambitions outstripped his judgment, and he declared war on the emperor in Rome. He led his loyal British troops across the Narrow Sea into Gaul and across Gaul into Italy.

Some say he defeated the Emperor of Rome, some say he was defeated by him; whatever happened, he died there in Aquilea, and his remaining troops brought home his armor and his Sword. Many men stayed in Gaul and settled along the edge of the Narrow Sea in what men call Less Britain. The rest returned to Wales. His son Constantius ruled after him and was the ancestor of Constans, who was murdered by Vortigern, and of Ambrosius, who was the first to reunite the kings of Britain, and of Uther, who just managed to hold the Saxons at bay, until Arthur should come.

"It was written in the stars, Merlin said in a soft voice that carried to every corner of the hall, that in the dark hour the Light of Britain should arise with a Sword of wondrous brilliance: Maximus' own Sword, hidden in darkness for a hundred years, waiting for the hand of Britain's greatest King to lift it once again into the light."

He stopped and let the silence hang.

"Corwin," I whispered, "you should be a bard."

He laughed. "I may have to be, unless my leg heals straight. Anyway, those are Merlin's words about the Sword. Durwen told me, and he was there with King Pellinore. He *was* studying to be a bard and had learned how to get things by heart in one hearing."

"Was?" I asked quickly.

Corwin sobered. "Yes, my lady. The poor lad died on the way home of his wound. It was stitched, but he opened it again by sitting a horse too soon, and against orders."

"But the Sword!" Elaine cried impatiently. "What can you tell us about that? Where was it? How did Prince Arthur get it? And when did they proclaim him King?"

"Merlin claimed the Sword lay under Lluden's Hill, where it had been left by Maximus' chief captain. He had brought it north from Wales when Elen, in her grief, banished it from her sight. It lay in darkness, Merlin said, protected by the god of the place, to be raised into the light by him who was born the rightful King of Britain. He invited all the lords present to ride there, that very night, and witness its lifting. What could Lot do? Every lord in the hall, from king to count to troop captain, would have given years off his life to witness Merlin's powers in person. Lot had no hope of being acclaimed King in that hall; his only hope was to join the throng on Lluden's Hill and hope that Arthur or Merlin would fail." He laughed and then slowly sobered. "King Pellinore took only Durwen with him, because, according to Durwen, he felt that the anointing of a new king should be witnessed by a bard. Now, I suppose, it is left to me to tell it."

He paused again and, closing his eyes, spoke softly. "So they took to horse and rode upstream along the river Eden. In the dark hours of the morning they came to the black island that sits hard by the ford. Lluden's Hill, the locals call it; it has been a sacred place time out of mind. Merlin led them up the slope to an old tunnel, hidden by undergrowth, and through it into a gigantic cave. So large it was, none could see its roof, nor its ending. Their torches shed a dim and smoky light, enough to glimpse the cold immensity of the place and feel the weight of dark shadows pressing down." Elaine and I shivered, in spite of ourselves, and made the sign against enchantment, although we were Christians. "Forty men had followed Merlin, and they all stood within the cave, shuffling and whispering, hearing their own voices speak back to them from the living rock; a place haunted, Durwen swore, with the spirits of the Elder past. Merlin stood up before them, a black shadow in the darkness. 'Look before you,' he cried, 'and see the Sword of Maximus!' And there it was, in the middle of the vast cavern, stuck into the cleft of a huge rock. There it was; where a moment before they had seen nothing, now they saw the split rock, the dark shaft rising, the dim glow of the hilt seeming to float in the very air. Merlin beckoned, they moved closer, the bravest among them trembling. The scabbard was of some ancient silken fabric, embroidered with the crude marks of the Old Tongue that Britons spoke before the Romans came. Merlin raised high a torch that all might see the writing: 'WHOSO LIFTS THIS SWORD FROM THE STONE IS RIGHTWISE BORN KING OF ALL THE BRITONS.' He read it out in a voice of dread, and the echoes circled, chilling the soul. 'rightwise born ... rightwise born ... King of all the Britons.' "

"Corwin!" Elaine quavered, gripping my arm.

His eyes were closed. He did not even hear her. "No one dared to breathe. The Sword stood in its dark sheath, dull and cold, and all around the air stank with the sweat of fear. 'Let him who dares touch the Sword,' Merlin called out. But no one moved. At last King Lot stepped forward. 'I am fitter than any man here to be High King,' he proclaimed, 'but I distrust magicians.' Merlin folded his hands into his sleeves. 'Sir,' he said, 'there is no magic in this place but what the gods have bestowed in the Sword itself. I am powerless before it. If the Sword is yours, take it.' The lords held their breath as Lot reached out, put his hand to the hilt, and pulled."

Corwin opened his eyes and stared at us. "Then was the sacred silence rent with a mighty yell, for the Sword did not budge an iota, but Lot's hand was burned, the flesh seared across the palm where it had held the hilt. He withdrew his hand, white-faced with pain, and cursed Merlin for a lying, two-faced bastard." Elaine and I both gasped at such outrageous foolhardiness, but Corwin hardly paused for breath. "The company shrank back, afrighted. Someone called out, 'Let the boy try! Where's Ector's fosterling?' Arthur was pushed forward, and seeing that there was no way out of it, he stood straight as a spear before Merlin the Enchanter. 'Is it for me?' he asked the great magician. 'If you tell me to, I shall try it.'

"Oh, how brave he is!" Elaine gasped.

"How so," I countered, "when he has known Merlin his entire life? If there is not trust between them yet—"

"Oh, shut up, Gwen! You ruin everything!"

"Merlin told him," Corwin went on, ignoring us both, " 'it is yours, my lord King. It was made for your hand, even before it was made for Maximus.' So the lad went forward and put his hand to the hilt, and the great Sword slid as sweetly out of the sheath as a knife through butter. The torchlight caught the blade, setting it aglow; as he lifted it into the light, the great jewel in the hilt blazed into life. A huge emerald, hidden in the dark, struck its green fire into every soul and brought them all to their knees. Life! it signaled. Victory! As Arthur held it aloft he seemed to grow taller before their eyes. His face shone in the reflected glory of the Sword, a face full of pride and fierce determination. 'I shall call it *Excalibur*,' he said, which in the Old Tongue means 'unconquered.' Then every lord came and knelt before him to pay homage and receive his blessing. Lot was last, but he spoke well and promised faithful service. So they made him their King in that sacred place, King of all the Britons, and carried him outside as dawn broke in the east. And behind in the cavern the rock lay split in two halves, and the scabbard crumbled into dust, when the Sword was freed."

Elaine's eyes were as large as goose eggs. The magnificence of her hero had been amply confirmed.

"That's not the end." Corwin smiled. "While Durwen was busy spinning phrases in his head to recite to me, others among the lords, including Cyndeg and Aguisel, were grumbling that the whole thing had been a setup. Merlin had done nothing but lead them to the Sword. They might have sworn to follow the boy who held that Sword, but they wanted proof that Merlin's powers were behind him. The lifting of the Sword was not enough; they wanted more."

"What fools men are!" I breathed.

"And Merlin heard them. As they made ready to depart, with the new King at their head, Merlin turned around in the saddle and raised his arms. A thunderous crack rent the sky, a flash of fire burst forth, and the hillside above the cave came down. Trees bent double, horses bolted and men bellowed in fear, but Merlin sat and calmly watched Lluden's Hill slide into a mountain of rubble. When the last stone had tumbled to a stop at Merlin's feet, he coolly turned and surveyed the doubters, who shook before his gaze. Then he reined in and rode behind Arthur back to camp."

We brought Corwin a flask of honey mead and thanked him sincerely for his tale. Elaine was speechless for a while, but soon she found her tongue.

"And what does King Arthur look like?" she asked eagerly. "Do tell us."

Corwin looked a little blank. "What do you mean, my lady?"

"I mean, is he dark or fair? Tall or short? Lean or heavy?"

Corwin smiled and said to me, "It seems the young princess is not without ambition." I winked at a scarlet Elaine as he continued. "Well, from what I saw of him, he is tall for his age and slender for a warrior, but he is young yet. He is an excellent swordsman, near the best I have seen. What else? Let me see, brown hair, brown eyes, a clear skin with a serious expression, well featured, with a look of Uther about him, and when he was young Uther was considered handsome by all the ladies of the land." Then Corwin's gaze grew distant, and his voice pensive. "But I think what is most impressive about him is something that I cannot put into words. Men call it poise, or inner peace, or wisdom, or strength, or grace of bearing, but it is all those and more; he is a man in harmony with himself. He has a mission. He knows who he is."

"He must be a born leader," I said thoughtfully, "for the men he commands are seasoned warriors and kings in their own right. Sword or no sword, men like King Pellinore and my brother Gwarthgydd would not follow a mere boy."

"Indeed," Corwin agreed. "And it isn't due to Merlin's magic, either. For Merlin disappeared after the lifting of the Sword and hasn't been seen since. Yet the army is off after Colgrin, with King Arthur at its head."

"He will beat the Saxons," Elaine said confidently, "and drive them from our shores forever."

"It will be a miracle indeed if he does that," Corwin replied. "The Saxons have been living on the Shore since Vortigern first invited them, fifty years ago. There are children your age, my young lady, whose grandfathers were born in Britain. Small wonder they consider it their home."

"But we were here first," Elaine objected.

"We Welsh?" I asked her. "Or we British? We are led by a descendant of Maximus, who was a Roman and a foreigner. The Celts were here before the Romans, and the Ancients before the Celts. No one knows who was here before the Ancients. Perhaps the Saxons are next."

"That's treason!" Elaine cried, tears springing to her eyes. "Gwen, I will never forgive you unless you take it back! How can you say such a thing?" Even Corwin looked shocked.

"If it isn't possible to drive the Saxons out—and where, indeed, can they go? —then it will be necessary to treat with them. Yes, I know the old saying: A treaty with a Saxon is smoke in the wind, but it seems to me it's the strongest sword that prevails. Perhaps what Merlin said is true and that Arthur's Sword is the strongest. Then we shall have peace with the Saxons." I could see that they both were calmer, and Elaine was on the verge of forgiving me. "Who knows? In two hundred years perhaps even the Saxons will be British."

Elaine gasped in horror and began to berate me; Corwin looked afraid.

"My lady Guinevere, it is not my place to say so, but these are not matters that should concern young maids. These are high matters, and beyond such as me; they are better left to the king's council chamber. You have a mind, my lady, which may bring you grief if you give it tongue. Such thoughts are better left unspoken."

It was good advice. I did not tell him that it was talk in the king's council chamber that had given rise to these thoughts, voiced here for the first time. I accepted his rebuke, apologized to Elaine, and kept my thoughts to myself thereafter. It was twenty years before I found a mind receptive to these thoughts: a man who accepted them and went beyond them, who believed in compromise and in the value of other cultures besides his own, a man who envisioned the entire civilized world as one community. That man was Mordred.

4 ✸ The Sin

During the next five years King Pellinore was often from home while Arthur's new Kingdom fought for its fledgling life. The Saxons had been soundly defeated at Caer Eden, and Colgrin their leader had died of wounds received on that field. But there were other war leaders eager to fill Colgrin's place. Caelwin, Colgrin's second-in-command, organized the East Saxons, treated with the Angles, and with their combined forces fought to establish a new beachhead along the eastern shores. If Lot of Lothian treated with them, it would split Britain in two.

And along the Saxon Shore arose a youth who dared to call himself King of the West Saxons: Cerdic the Aetheling, Eosa's son, who promised his people freedoms and rule by law, should they conquer Britain. I wondered at his temerity—was not Roman law good enough for the likes of him?

But Arthur led his troops to victory after victory, with great losses on the Saxon side and few on his own. Young as he was, older men granted him their respect, and hardened warriors deferred to his opinions, for there is no talisman luckier than victory, and he did not seem able to lose. Everywhere they were attacked, Britons fought bravely, from king to foot soldier, knowing that the High King would come to their aid with his invincible Sword, Excalibur, and his companion force of trained warriors.

Without fail Arthur came and conquered. By the time I was ten he was already a legend in his own land. He never lost so much as a skirmish. His name was a password for victory, and men said he had only to appear on the horizon for the Saxons to turn and flee.

Elaine believed every word she heard about him, and I was forced to stop my teasing under the pressure of her adoration. She even fasted the whole day of his coronation, while everyone else feasted. He was no longer our hope, she told me with earnest passion, he was our savior. And truly, I could not in good grace quarrel with her, for the kings of Britain hastened to unite behind this fearless warrior, and for the first time in men's memories Wales, Cornwall, Rheged, Lothian, and scores of lesser kingdoms felt a kinship with one another—we were all part of one realm.

This took time to achieve. Indeed, for the first year of his reign, Arthur was busy fighting stop-gap battles in the east, north, and southeast. He had been High King for over six months before the Saxons left him enough breathing space to get himself crowned. It was a Christian ceremony, and he was anointed by a Christian priest at Pentecost, but it was held in the old fighting fortress of Caerleon with a minimum of ceremony, because, in the King's own words, there was little time. Most of his attendants were his troops and nobles, although all the lords and ladies of the land had been invited. King Pellinore and Queen Alyse attended, for Caerleon, lying on a hill above the Severn, was but four days' journey south. It was April, and spring was early that year, so the roads were clear and they made good time. According to Elaine, Pellinore had intended to take only his soldiers with him, but the queen refused to be left behind. She claimed she didn't care if she had to sleep in a tent; she wanted to see the young High King crowned.

When she returned, she was the center of all our attention, and one afternoon, in an expansive mood, she gathered us all around her: her waiting women, Elaine and me, and our nurses, and she told us all about it.

It was not grand, she said, more a meeting among war leaders than a social event, but the High King's mother, the lady Ygraine, had come up from Cornwall and had spent much time with Alyse, one of the few queens close enough to attempt the journey. Ygraine still grieved for her lost Uther and looked pale and wasted. Her physician traveled with her, but it was Merlin who concocted her a brew that brought color to her cheeks and allowed her to attend the ceremony without exciting her son's attention.

"Merlin!" Elaine cried. "Was he there? Did you really see Merlin the Enchanter, Mother? Were you in the room with him? What does he look like?"

Queen Alyse laughed gently. "You young ones grew up on the tales of his doings, I see, and to you he is a creature of fable. But he is real enough, I assure you. And free of arrogance, for such a powerful man. Without him, young Arthur would not now be King."

"Saints preserve us!" Grannic cried, crossing herself, and Ailsa clutched the amulet at her breast.

"Is he very fearful, Mother?" Elaine whispered. "Did you see him use magic?"

"No, child. He came often to visit Ygraine. They are old friends. But he used no magic except what he put in the broth that gave her the strength to see her son crowned."

"Is he ugly, Mama?"

"Goodness, no. He is tall, of course, and dark. Black hair and eyes. You would think him old, but I do not. He is slender and quiet and does not say much. He listens to everything. They say the young King loves him as a father and depends upon him greatly. Not for fighting, of course. By his own admission Merlin is no swordsman. But for matters of state, I should imagine he is the wisest advisor a king could have."

"What was the coronation like, Mother? Did you have to stay in a tent? Did you get to see King Arthur? Is he handsome and fierce? Tell us!"

Alyse laid a gentle hand on Elaine's head, and I watched her eyes. They looked through Elaine to something beyond. "We were lodged in a house next to Ygraine's. It was a high honor, for there are few private dwellings there yet, although I hear the High King has plans for the place. Yes, I saw the High King at the ceremony and afterward, when he greeted his guests. He is just fourteen, but already an experienced war leader. You could see it in his eyes, his bearing, his sureness. He is—he is—" she paused, searching for the words to describe the youth she saw in her mind's eye. "He is tall, but not too tall, he is handsome, but not to swooning point. He has a look of Uther about him, but not his temper, God be praised. And by all accounts he is moderate in his habits." No one needed to remind us of Uther's reputation for womanizing. It was a saying that he had never slept alone. "But one doesn't see him in that way. What you see is singleness of purpose, of youth and strength and joy. He was born for this, Merlin said to Ygraine, and it seems he knows it." She sighed and smiled gently. "As a mother, I would want him for my son. Were I a girl again, I would want him for my husband."

Elaine caught my eye and sighed in deep satisfaction. Alyse continued her account of her visit and the nobles she saw, but for Elaine the rest was chaff. She had her fantasy of Arthur confirmed and was happy to bursting point.

* * *

Those were good years, those early ones. While Elaine and I studied Latin and Greek and figuring, learned stitching and weaving and housekeeping, raced along the rocky beaches on our ponies, and listened in on the king's councils when we could, Arthur was busy repairing the Kingdom's defenses, building roads and fortresses, setting up communication links of signals fires from hilltop to tor top, refurbishing ransacked towns and castles, restoring life and trust to the land. He traveled constantly from kingdom to kingdom, renewing treaties and helping lords with their local problems in return for their pledge to come to his call. Around him he gathered the young men of the kingdoms, nobles' sons, and forged them, through friendship, into a close-knit group. With the help of a king's son from Less Britain, who was a consummate horseman, Arthur sent to Gaul for fine, swift horses and crossed them with the strong, native breeds to get warhorses unsurpassed in power, speed, and intelligence. Arthur's mounted Companions became a swift, mobile cavalry and one of his deadliest weapons.

But as they say in Wales, every sun has its shadow. No one is immune from slander, and one day I heard a tale that wove a dark thread of evil into the fabric of the new King's glory. I was in my horse's box, rubbing him down after a ride and grooming his silken coat, a job I preferred to do myself than leave to a groom, when I heard men talking.

One of Pellinore's men spoke carelessly as he handed over his sweated horse; I had lingered long after my ride and no doubt they thought I had returned to the castle with Elaine.

"Ho there, Stannic, how goes it?"

"Well, young master, thank you kindly. You made good time. We weren't expecting you before sundown."

"I hurried from York," the trooper replied, and then their voices became muffled as they went together into the horse's stall. I was about to straighten up and slip out, when I caught the High King's name and the word "massacre." Quickly I crouched in the corner of the box and kept as still as I could. The trooper came out and lounged nearby in the aisle, speaking with the voice of one who delights in bearing bad news.

"They are talking about it all over York," he gloated. "Two hundred babies, they say, all boys, all newborns, set adrift in a fishing craft with the sail lashed to the tiller and the course set for the rocks. I got it from a man who got it from his sister, and she lives in Dunpelder."

Dunpelder! The capital of Lothian. Lot's city.

"Oh, he was in a rare fury was King Lot. Put yourself in his shoes, Stannic. You're away campaigning with the High King, your bride of eight months tucked safely away in your castle, with guards aplenty. You have left her with child, but what do you find when you return for her lying-in? A slender wife, an empty crib, a thin tale of an early birthing and a quick death. And all the while the place is buzzing with the rumors of a strong boy born six weeks ago, looking no more like Lot than a dragon does an eagle!"

Stannic mumbled something, and the trooper laughed. I wondered what this common little tale had to do with the High King.

"Yes, there was a child, all right. But she hid him well. She's a witch, you know, a proper sorceress as well as a beauty. I'd say she was capable of anything. Seduction and deception would come as natural as breathing to her. Oh, it's not Lot's child, that's for sure. Lot beat her till she was well nigh senseless but could get no truth from her. All York is full of the news."

"Is that why he killed the children?" Stannic asked. "To find the boy?"

"Did I say it was Lot's doing? The babe had other enemies. Can't you guess whose child it was?"

"Her bath slave? The captain of the guard?"

The trooper paused, and I feared he would leave his tale unfinished, but he had only stopped to drain his hip flask, for I heard him push the stopper in and belch.

"Listen, Stannic," he continued, but very softly, and a curious, stealthy quality in his voice sent a shiver of fear down my spine; I crept to the front of the box to hear. "Can't you guess the reason for Lot's fury? No, no, if it had just been the queen's bastard, he'd have tossed it out, not sought to kill it. You never heard the rumors then? There was talk after Caer Eden about them. Morgause and Arthur, I mean. Before she was married to Lot, and before he was proclaimed King Uther's son." His voice fell to a hoarse whisper, and I strained to catch it. "The young prince shared her bed there, they say, his first woman, the night of his victory. And that she carried his child within her when she wed Lot soon after. You can be sure Lot had heard the rumors and wanted no Dragon chick in his nest, bastard or not."

"Does the High King know?" Stannic asked, coming out of the box.

"Well, that's the question of the hour, isn't it? Someone's troops invaded the city and slayed every newborn male child. Every house was searched. Babies dragged from their mothers' breasts, lifted sleeping from their cradles, and thrown into an open boat. They said you could hear the cries of those babies for hours after the boat was out of sight, and of course the wailings of the mothers for days on end . . . No, none survived. The bodies all came in on the tide three days ago."

"Are you suggesting—" Stannic's voice was shaking, "—are you suggesting they were *royal* troops?"

"Who knows? They wore no badge. And it stands to reason the King would want to kill the child. What a hostage to his future that would be, a bastard son raised by the Witch of Lothian!"

"Not this King," Stannic whispered. "He's but a youth yet. He's no evil in him."

"And who stands behind him at his right hand but Merlin the Enchanter, master of the black arts? Don't tell me, my man, it isn't possible. With kings, anything is possible. The north country is already laying the blame at Arthur's door. York is divided. In the south, they'll probably blame Lot."

"I blame the Witch herself!" Stannic cried, and the trooper laughed.

"Well, no doubt, she is the root of all the trouble. So beautiful, they say, she turns men's wits. But would she give the order to murder innocent children?"

"She might, to safeguard the boy. Bastards have come to power before now. Didn't you say Lot had beaten her in a temper? Well, I've known women who would do any evil thing to cover the tracks of a lie. If she'd hidden the baby well, as you said, she could slay the city's children and keep her dangerous son safe. That would cool the king's anger and still the wagging tongues."

"Hmmm. Perhaps, if you think a woman capable of murdering children. I don't know. But it was a terrible, black deed, and the blame for it must settle somewhere."

"I pray the Goddess it does not settle on the young King."

"Even if it doesn't, he will suffer for it. How would you like a crafty wolf like Lot murdering a host of innocents just to kill yours? Leave you with a bad taste in your mouth, wouldn't it? Leave you feeling a little unclean?"

I believe I screamed in horror, but my hands were over my mouth, and they were walking away together, so they did not hear me. The trooper left, but Stannic came back and walked down the aisle, checking the horses. I was pressed frozen against the door, and he did not see me. He doused the oil lamp, closed the door, and went out. I went to my dozing horse and wrapped my arms around his neck, burying my face in his rough mane to hide my tears.

I knew, as the trooper told the story, that there was more to it than he was telling, or perhaps than he knew, and when he said the word "unclean" I knew suddenly what it was. Morgause was Uther's bastard daughter, born before he married the Queen Ygraine. *She was Uther's daughter. Arthur's sister.* I crossed myself quickly as I thought the unclean thought. It had been a sin time out of mind. Could it be true? Could the High King have done such a thing? I remembered the tales that had circulated among the returning wounded at that time, that the prince was kept ignorant of his birth, at Uther's wish, until Uther proclaimed him on his deathbed. That was the day after the battle, when they celebrated the victory. Was it possible, then, that when he went to Morgause he did not know who he was?

But if he sinned in innocence, he must have realized the truth the next day, when Uther acknowledged him. Hadn't Corwin described him as dazed and grim soon after the announcement? Here was a motive for murder stronger than any the trooper had named. Such a son would be a blight upon his honor, a smear across his good name, as well as a threat to his power. Lesser men had done greater evil for smaller sins than that!

I found myself shaking badly. There seemed no way out of the dilemma. Either Arthur was guilty of incest or of murder, and perhaps of both. Our new King, our stainless, shining hope, would bear forever the taint of evil, once the news got out.

I realized suddenly that the trooper had come home to tell the news at the council table, and I straightened and stilled my trembling. I would dampen my clothing in the horse's trough and feign illness, so Elaine could not persuade me to go out on the turret and eavesdrop tonight. Someday she might find out, and if the story of the massacre was spreading across Britain with the speed it was spreading across Wales, then it was likely she would hear it from someone, but it wasn't going to be me. Elaine was my only friend, and I was going to keep her Arthur untarnished for her.

5 ✹ The Gift

Queen Alyse and her ladies-in-waiting sat stitching and dozing in the queen's garden, enjoying the soft sea breeze and the warming sun of midmorning. The winter had been a hard one, and more than one of the women nursed a lingering cough. It was luxury to spend the day outside the cold castle walls, delighting in the sun, the smells of new growth, and the early birdsong.

It was the first of May and my thirteenth birthday. Father Martin released us early from our lessons, praising our progress and pretending he didn't know it was my birthday. There were celebrations in the village, where maids plaited wildflowers into their hair and danced with the young men, and the smoke from their feast fires drifted up the hill to our castle. This was Beltane, a day sacred to the Goddess, and while King Pellinore and Queen Alyse kept a Christian household, most Welshmen honored the Mother as well as Christ and observed her holy days.

I had been looking forward to this day for a long time, because I was sure that on this day God would make me a woman. I had prayed so hard and tried so earnestly to keep all His commandments, obeying even the most stringent of the rules set down by Queen Alyse for ladylike behavior.

And more than that, I had learned, at great cost to my pride, to take my appointed place in Elaine's shadow. When she was willful I did not thwart her, but found some politic way, if I could, to temper her headstrong ways and yet avoid her anger. When I failed, and her silly schemes ended in disaster, I learned to hold my tongue when I was blamed. Once when Elaine and I sneaked down to the buttery to steal the new cream from jugs just set out, the cook caught us and scolded us roundly for our greed. Knowing from long experience whose idea it was, she chided Elaine for her appetite and threatened to tell the queen. That very morning

Alyse had lectured Elaine about her fondness for sweets and cream, so Elaine turned around and blamed the adventure on me. Because I knew I would pay for it well if I denied it, I confessed, and from then on Alyse concluded that it was I who was responsible for every lump of sugar that went missing from the storerooms.

When there was punishment, I took it. Afterward, Elaine would give me a sweet apology and a promise of better behavior. And if Alyse frowned and scowled and called me a young fool, I could always rely on Pellinore's forgiveness. He could not bear to see me out of temper and would tease me back to good humor with all the good-hearted boisterousness in his generous nature.

For these sacrifices, I was sure God would answer my prayer. Although Elaine was a year younger than I was, she had already grown round breasts and hips and had passed her menarche. All I had done was grow taller. I was taller now than Queen Alyse, but straight as a boy, with no sign that my body would ever change. But I was sure God had heard my prayers. Father Martin said He paid special attention to the requests of virgins.

Queen Alyse and her ladies had made us each a new dress to celebrate the day, and we hurried to change into them. Elaine's was made of a sky-blue cloth, soft and fine, that matched her eyes exactly. It had a high belt and rounded throat, accentuating her budding figure. She looked beautiful. Mine was a soft, spring green, the color of new leaves cut out of silk that must have come from the warm lands far to the south. The lace at the throat was a sign of love and honor, for lace was rare in Britain and very costly. But the dress fit like a glove and could not hide the straightness of my frame. Next to Elaine, I looked like one of Alyse's garden scarecrows.

"Gwen!" Elaine gasped. I turned to find her staring at me in distress.

"What's the matter?"

She shook her head angrily. "You have no right to outshine me!" she blurted. "Change your dress!"

"What? What are you talking about?"

"You know full well what I am talking about! You have been admiring yourself in the bronze half the morning! I mean it, I will not be outdone!"

"Outdone, indeed!" I retorted. "It ill becomes you to mock me, Elaine. Just because you look like a woman of twenty, and I—I—I will grow a shape someday and find a husband, just wait and see!"

"Too soon for me!" she cried, in tears.

"Good heavens, Elaine! Are you blind? Come and look at yourself! You look fit to be courted by one of the High King's Companions!"

This was the highest compliment I could think of, for the King's Companions were the finest men in all the land. But it did not please her; she scowled and turned away. I did not dream, then, of Elaine's ambition.

"Fat chance I shall have of ever courting anybody, Gwen, until you are married. Who will look at little Elaine, standing in Guinevere's shadow?"

I grabbed her arm. "What nonsense is this? You are Pellinore's daughter! Have some sense, Elaine!"

But she pulled away angrily. "Leave me alone! You'd just better leave me alone!" And she fled out the door and down the corridor before I could stop her.

"What have I done?" I cried to Ailsa, who bent to retrieve the comb Elaine had thrown aside. "What did I say? Do you know what is the matter?"

"Indeed"—she smiled—"but pay it no mind, my lady. It's an illness without a cure."

"Well, whatever is amiss?" I demanded. "Tell me!"

She looked up slowly, her eyes narrowing in laughter. "Be easy, my lady. If you don't know yet, time will tell you. Go on down to her now and be kind to her. You can bring her around, if you try."

I composed myself as best I could and went down to the garden, where I knew the queen was waiting for us. Elaine was there before me, but she kept her eyes in her lap and did not greet me. The conversation centered on the big event of the day, which was Pellinore's return from King Arthur's court. He was bringing me a special birthday gift, the messenger had said, but it was a great secret. Not even Alyse knew what it was.

Pellinore had been gone three months with his troops of fighting men, helping the High King repair the defenses along the Saxon Shore. Rumor had it they had been with Arthur when they defeated a Saxon force newly landed in longboats. The Saxons had been many in number, and the High King's force was small, only Pellinore's foot soldiers and those of two lesser lords of the Summer Country, but the Saxons had been without horses, and Arthur's Companions had demolished them. The young knight from Less Britain, Lancelot of Lanascol, who had bred and trained the horses, had been honored at the victory feast. The

High King graciously gave him credit for the victory and made him first among the Companions, his second-in-command. The fact is, he already was in all but name, for having no kin in Britain, he of necessity lodged and traveled with the High King, and they had become close friends.

Now the messenger had said the King had moved north to York, and Pellinore was coming home for what we all hoped was a long stay, bringing with him a surprise.

I picked up the piece of stitchery I was working on and listened almost absentmindedly to the women talking, my thoughts full of womanhood and distress at Elaine's sudden temper. Would she never cease her childish sulking and be my friend again?

"Melwas is King of the Summer Country," Alyse was saying, "although they say it is his sister Seulte who rules there. She claims to be a witch, but those who live there on Ynys Witrin say her foul temper is only bitterness at her inability to find a husband." Leave it to Alyse, I thought, to touch unerringly on Elaine's sorest spot.

"Isn't there a shrine to the Good Goddess on Ynys Witrin?" Elaine asked swiftly, to divert her mother. "I'm sure I heard it somewhere, but I thought there was a monastery there, too. How can there be both?"

"My goodness, Elaine, how do you get your information? You have never been to the Summer Country, and I am sure I did not know anything about it until Pellinore spent so much time there in the last year."

Of course we had got the information by eavesdropping. I caught Elaine's quick, warning glance and hid a smile. She turned an innocent face to her mother. "I don't know, Mother, I must have picked it up at the stables, I guess. Sometimes the men talk when they don't know young maids are about."

A chill of horror shot through me, and I almost gasped, reminded of the trooper from York. Was it possible Elaine knew the wretched tale, or had it merely been an arrow in the dark? I bent low over my work to hide my face.

"Ah, well, little pitchers have big ears. Yes, Avalon lies on Ynys Witrin below Melwas' fortress, the Christian monastery farther up the Tor. The monks and the Ladies of the Lake get along well enough. They are all in the service of the Divine. The priestesses are skilled in the healing arts, as the monks are in prayer and meditation. There has been no trouble there, at any rate. The trouble has all come from Melwas. He is young and handsome and is a likable enough fellow, I gather, but he has rather an eye for the girls in training. I understand he has ruined more than one pretty acolyte, and he is only twenty."

"Perhaps," one of her ladies said, "it is time for him to marry."

"No doubt it is, Cissa. But his sister stands in his way. No one is good enough for the lady Seulte, although I daresay Melwas himself is not so choosy. But he will not cross his sister, who feeds him full of praise and ambition, and so he bides by her will. Pellinore fears there will be more trouble in that quarter for some time."

"But at least it's only woman trouble," Leonora said.

"Perhaps," said Cissa, "he should look farther north for his bride." She turned and smiled at Elaine, who colored. I shot Elaine a triumphant glance, but she ignored me.

Alyse paused and looked at both of us thoughtfully. "Perhaps," she said, "but there is time yet. And I haven't told you the big news." She put down her work and gathered our attention. "I expect we will hear the details when King Pellinore comes home tonight, but I don't see why I can't tell you now what I know of it. As you know, the High King has been looking to build a fortress for his troops for some time. Caerleon, reinforced though it is, is not big enough. He has collected many men who follow him, not to mention the horses, and there are no hill forts large enough to accommodate his household. So a month ago they broke ground at a new site."

This set the ladies chattering with delight. At last the kingdom would have a center, a court that did not have to migrate from kingdom to kingdom, a place Arthur could call his own.

"It is in the Summer Country, which is what made me think of Melwas," Alyse continued. "On a high tor, flat-topped and long-sloped, within sight of the signal fires on Ynys Witrin. It sits near the river Camel, and there is a spring near the summit. It is rumored that before winter the fortifications will be complete, and lodging for the troops and horses ready. The castle, of course, will take longer."

What need had Arthur of a castle, I thought to myself, if he had good fortifications and lodgings for troops and horses? For five years he had done without either consistently and was still victorious wherever he raised his Sword.

"This is good news indeed, my lady," Cissa cried. "And perhaps, in two or three years, when he has built a home to bring a bride to, the High King will marry at last." It had long been a worry among my lady's maids, and I suspect among many of the ladies of the land, that the young King had not yet given a thought to marriage. He was now eighteen, well grown, well favored, war-hardened, and beyond all doubt the most eligible bachelor in the land.

Queen Alyse laughed in delight. "Cissa, my dear, you anticipate me. The new court at Caer Camel was but half my news. Hear this. The High King is betrothed and will wed come September."

I happened to be looking at Elaine and saw her blanch. She bent her head quickly, but I had seen tears forming in her eyes. With the swiftness of a lighting flash, I understood at last.

"Who is it, my lady?" the ladies were asking with eagerness. "Who backed her? What is her family?"

Queen Alyse took time to hush them, and Elaine struggled valiantly to compose her features. "She is the daughter of the Earl of Ifray, who was killed in battle at Duke Cador's side four years ago. Her mother died at her birth, and she has been raised in Cador's household since her father's death. Remember that the High King made Cador of Cornwall his heir until a prince should be born. And Cador is on excellent terms with his stepmother, the queen Ygraine." The women nodded solemnly to one another. There were no stronger backers in the land than the High King's mother and his heir-apparent, excepting only Merlin.

"She is sixteen," the queen continued, "and quite pretty, by all accounts. She has had speech once or twice with the High King." At least they know one another." Alyse had married Pellinore for love, which was almost unheard of at that time, and firmly believed that young maids should not be given in marriage to strangers. "And her name," Alyse said, "is Guenwyvar." They all gasped in surprise and then looked at me sidelong, as if I had lost by a near miss.

"Lord be praised," Leonora murmured. "At last we shall have a Queen and Arthur's line shall be established."

"Yes," the queen continued. "And it has been in my mind, that after the building at Caer Camel is finished, the High King and his Queen will want company at court, and his Companions may want wives, if the wars allow. It may be we shall move to the Summer Country in two years' time." The ladies looked at us and smiled knowingly.

Elaine's misery was heartbreaking to see, but no one seemed to notice it but I. As soon as I could, I made some excuse to leave, and Elaine followed me willingly. We fled to our room, and Elaine burst into sobs upon her bed. I sat beside her and stroked her fair hair. It was the color of ripe grain, dark gold and glowing.

Much lovelier, to my mind, than my white-gold hair, a childhood color I had yet to outgrow, and which always made strangers stare.

"I'm sorry, Elaine. I had no idea. I knew you idolized him; he has been your hero since tales about him first started to go round. But I never knew you really—expected to—"

"Oh, stop!" Elaine sobbed. "I knew it was hopeless, but I couldn't help it! I knew this would happen! And now Mother thinks to marry us off to his Companions!"

"Would that not be an honor?" I asked her. "Surely any maid chosen by the Companions would be among the first in Britain."

"I don't care! Oh, Gwen, it would be too awful! To be there in the High King's court and married to someone else. I couldn't stand it! And I don't *want* to marry anyone else! I shall never marry! Never!"

I tried to soothe her and calm her, but she so enjoyed her weeping fit that she ceased to fight for control and grew hysterical. It took Grannic and Ailsa both to calm her, with cold cloths to her head and warm blankets on her body. This was Elaine at her most tiresome; she often enjoyed the complete release of her emotions, always suffering dreadfully for it afterward, with headaches that could last days, but in a strange way I did not understand, she enjoyed the suffering, too.

I left her to the nurses, who calmed her to sleep, and went to the stables. My brown gelding Peleth was beyond his best years, which is why King Pellinore had taken him from a trooper and given him to me. But he was willing and had been an athlete in his prime, and I had taught him a new skill in his old age: I had taught him to jump. We had begun with natural barriers on the woodland trails: downed trees, rain-washed boulders, low walls, but these became easy with practice, and lately I had secretly built obstacles from branches, rocks, and greens, some wide and some tall, and he learned to take them all with ease. It was a wonderful feeling, flying through the air with the wind whipping my hair, and Peleth loved it.

I was not yet a woman; I checked before I went out, but the day was only half spent, and there was still time. We practiced jumping until he took all his fences perfectly, and then went for a gallop along the beach. The day was mild and clear, and the sea spray cold. We returned as the sun dipped toward the hilltops, splashed with seawater, sand, and mud, and very tired and happy. I did not go in the stable, but left him with the groom, for I knew I was late and had probably been missed.

Ailsa was in a panic. "My lady, where in the name of all the saints and devils have you been? King Pellinore has returned, and we are bidden to dinner! And look at you! You've torn your tunic, God knows on what"—she crossed herself quickly—"and your leggings are filthy!"

I laughed as she tugged the tunic off. "This is nothing, Ailsa. You should see Peleth!"

"What will become of you!" she wailed. "You're as wild as an Irish elf and shall never find a husband!"

She had touched inadvertently on my innermost fear, and I felt the gaiety drain from my body.

Ailsa saw it and began to croon lovingly. "That's just my way of talking, my lady. Don't pay any heed to a silly old woman. You're as lovely as a summer's eve, and as soon as the Good Lady blesses you with your monthlies, there's not a prince in the land who won't be knocking at King Pellinore's door for your hand. Mark my words, my lady. Remember what the witch foretold. First in the land will you be."

A sob rose in my throat, but I swallowed it back. Giselda's prophecy! It was clear to me now. The witch had been right. I might be flat-chested forever, a spinster and a burden in my old age, but no matter. The first in the land bore my name.

I had missed King Pellinore's arrival, and remembering that the feast tonight was held in my honor, I lifted my skirts and raced down to the greeting hall. I was surprised to see that Elaine had recovered enough to join the ladies seated about the great log fire. Usually she was long abed after such weeping. I supposed she had been made to join the birthday celebration; she looked pale and unhappy.

King Pellinore stood beside the queen's chair, holding Alyse's hand. His affection for her was a true one, and he never strove to hide it. He had two visitors with him, a man and a youth, but they stood with their backs to me, facing the fire, so I came upon them unawares.

"Ah, here's Gwen!" the king cried, smiling kindly at me.

I curtsied low before him. "Please forgive me, gracious king. We are so happy to see you safely returned to us, and I did not mean to be late. It was—"

He laughed and raised me, hugging me warmly. "The horses, no doubt. What else? Come, see who I have brought back with me from court."

I turned and faced two tanned, black-haired warriors, no taller than myself, with thick, strong bodies and dark pelts of hair along their arms. The younger of the two, after a wide-eyed glance at me, studied the floor; the elder grinned at me, his black eyes sparkling.

"Gwarthgydd!" I gasped, throwing myself into his arms. "Oh, Gwarthgydd, my brother!"

He laughed and swung me around. "Little Guinevere, I'd not have known you! Look at you, taller than me, by Mithra! You are a beauty, Gwen, there's no denying it." He turned to the youth beside him. "This will be something to tell your mother, Gwillim, won't it?"

"Gwillim!" I cried, staring at him. I had not recognized him at all. Of course he was taller, but that wasn't it. He was fourteen, had grown a beard and moustache, and looked at me with the eyes of a stranger. But I hugged him nevertheless. We had been playmates once. He stiffened and nearly fell to one knee, but restrained himself.

"Oh, Gwillim, I am so glad to see you! How came you to be here? Have you been with the High King? Did you not stop at Northgallis? Did you come on to see me?"

Gwillim was clearly speechless, so Gwarthgydd replied. "To see you, dear sister, and to honor King Pellinore, who invited us most kindly. And to show Gwillim his first sight of the sea." His glance flicked ever so slightly toward the moody Elaine, and I noticed that Pellinore was smiling at Alyse. "And to show Gwillim the beauties of Gwynedd," he finished politely. I understood instantly. They had come to inspect Elaine.

King Pellinore was clearly delighted, but Queen Alyse did not return his smiles. After the conversation in the garden I understood she had much higher ambitions for her daughter than marriage to a Welsh lord. Everyone was polite, of course, and conversation never lagged. King Pellinore's table was unlike any other I had heard of—it was round. The beauty of this arrangement was that it allowed everyone to see and talk to everyone else. There were long trestle tables and benches, as well, which were used to feast troops after victories of importance, or on high holy days, but always the family sat at the round table.

There was much toasting my health, and conversation about the Saxon wars, which was supposed to be above the ladies' heads, but which I listened to avidly. Elaine kept her eyes on her plate like any shy, young maid being courted for the first time. But I knew it was not modesty but misery that was blanketing her high spirits. And Gwillim, who should at least have shown some inter-

est, if only curiosity, about the girl his father offered for, either
looked at his own plate or looked at me. Try though I might, I
could not engage him in conversation. He only responded "Yes,
my lady" or "No, my lady" or, when I referred to the time we had
found the wild ponies, "I pray you won't mention it, my lady."
What could one do? At least Gwarthgydd had news of home. He
and all his brothers were in the High King's service now, and he
had nothing but praise for Arthur. What a leader! Calm, wise, pur-
poseful, never a hasty move or an unplanned foray; gentle with
women, just with men, ruthless with his enemies. He was full of
laughter and good humor; men feared his rare anger; he fought
not with heat but with unswerving, cold purpose.

When I could get him off the subject of Arthur, he told me of
home. He had married two of his daughters off and seemed glad
to be rid of them. His brothers had large families, more than the
King's house at Cameliard could hold, and lived on their own
lands. That left him with Glynis, two young daughters, Gwillim
and his two older sons, who took turns soldiering and tending the
kingdom of Northgallis. I was still remembered there, he said.
Never had the black Celts of our family produced anyone so fair.
I nodded toward the blond Alyse, my mother's sister, and her
daughter, the fair Elaine. Gwarth smiled. Yes, he said, everyone
knew where it came from, and he wouldn't mind at all having another fair maid in Northgallis. I felt obliged to tell him it looked
unlikely. He glanced unhappily at Gwillim and agreed.

"King Pellinore seems pleased with the match, though."

"Probably because it means his precious daughter would be
next door," I told him. "But I assure you, Gwarth, the queen feels
strongly that her daughter will not be forced into a marriage
against her will—and the lady Elaine has a strong will."

"Hmmmm. Well, I expect you're right. I can't say Gwill cares
at all. Perhaps it's just as well. He won't look at anyone but you,
Gwen. He never has."

I blushed. It was absurd. Gwillim was my nephew! I told
Gwarth how happy I was to see them both and that King Pellinore
could not have brought me a better birthday present.

He laughed aloud. "We're not your present, Gwen. King
Pellinore has brought you a rare gift, more precious than any
Welsh prince could ever be to you."

Pellinore heard him and rose. "I confess that the High King Arthur has done me a great honor. In return for my services in the
last battle, he asked me to name anything I wished, and if it was
in his power to give it me, he would." I saw heads turn and nod

at this extraordinary generosity. King Pellinore smiled. "I thought of the young lass I keep in my care and told the High King I wished to bring a birthday gift to my ward. I asked him for a mare from his own stables."

I gasped, and everyone stared. Such a gift was unheard of! All of the fine horses young Lancelot imported from Gaul, and their colts and fillies, were kept for training or for breeding stock. None had ever left the High King's stables. And mares were prized above all. I stared at Pellinore in amazement.

"Did—did he agree?" I whispered.

Pellinore laughed. "The mare is in the stables now," he said gently. "The High King keeps his promises."

I could barely contain my excitement. If she'd been stabled as soon as Pellinore arrived, she must have been in the barn when Peleth and I returned from our ride! I berated myself for not having gone in to tend the horse myself—I could have seen her then. As it was, I would not be allowed to go out until morning.

"Oh, dearest Pellinore!" I cried, jumping from my seat and running into his arms. "How can I ever thank you enough! What is she like? Her color, her stride, her spirits? Did anyone ride her on the journey home? Where is he, that I may ask?"

King Pellinore laughed and sat me on his lap, just the way my father had been wont to do when I was small. "No one rode her, young lady. She is yours. She's a filly, but two years old, and a dark dappled gray. But she will be as white as the High King's charger one day, you may be sure. She is not fully trained—I leave that to you—but what lessons she has had, she has had from the best. Young Lancelot bred her and trained her himself, and a finer hand with a horse I never hope to see. He hated to part with her and was sure I was exaggerating your skill." He pinched my cheek. "I told him you rode bareback, as he does himself, and flew like the west wind over whatever lay in your path." I blushed violently; I had thought my jumping was a secret. "He said to me, 'There's a maid after my own heart' and let me take the mare. You may see her in the morning, Gwen. Happy birthday."

I was beside myself with joy and anticipation. When dinner was over, I kissed Gwarth and Gwillim good night, paid my respects to Queen Alyse, and flew upstairs to my room. Elaine was sullen, whether with jealousy over my great gift or with a headache from her weeping, I knew not, and I cared not. A mare from the High King's stables! It was too wonderful to be true! I said my evening prayers in a hurry. God had not made me a woman that day, after all, but now I hardly cared.

* * *

I was up at dawn, dressed quietly in my doeskin leggings, crept out without waking Elaine or the nurses, and raced to the stables.

Stannic was up, and he grinned to see me, not surprised. "This way, my lady. I gave her the corner box. It's the biggest and she can look out over the meadow."

I stopped at the door and held my breath. She was a beauty! Tall, slender, straight legs, long, arched neck, flat croup, tail held high. She was looking out her window when I came up but, hearing my step, swung around to see me. Her face was lovely: broad in the forehead but narrow in the muzzle, with fine, large dark eyes.

"Sweet Mary," I whispered, opening the door a crack and slipping in. She was taller than I was, much taller than the Welsh mountain ponies I had grown up on, but lighter and finer than Peleth. Her coat was a dark dappled gray, with black legs, black mane and tail, and dark muzzle. I spoke to her softly, crooning an old Welsh tune, and held out my hand. She was nervous at first, but then stood calmly and let me approach. When I was near, she lowered her head and put her soft muzzle in my hand. Clearly, she had been brought up with no fear of men, which meant she had been well treated always. I stroked her gently, and she nuzzled me in return.

I slipped a halter on her and led her from the stall. She moved daintily, careful where she put her feet. I guessed she would be surefooted on rough ground. She did not look heavy enough to carry a soldier, but she must at least have carried Lancelot, so I was not afraid to mount her. I refused the bridle Stannic proffered, although it was very fine, with silver worked on the browband. She was only two, and likely tender-mouthed.

"Give me a leg up, Stannic."

"My lady," he protested, "surely you're not going to try her without a bridle. You'll not have control!"

"I have the halter and the rope. I can spin her in a circle if she looks to bolt. Have no fear."

My eagerness made me impatient, and I was ready to climb the fence to mount her, but Stannic helped me against his better judgment.

How can I describe what it felt like to be astride of her? She was light and quick, she felt every shift of my seat, every touch of my leg. She quivered with eagerness, but when I stroked her neck and talked to her, she calmed under my touch. I let her walk around the stableyard and then onto the track that led down the gentle valley toward the sea road. It was a lovely spring morning, with dew on the grass and a cool mist rising. The sun was up, rose pink through the haze, and the hills were alive with birdsong. The filly danced along the track, swinging this way and that, pulling at the rope, wanting her head. I denied it to her, and she did not fight me, but bent her neck gracefully and walked on. She had been handled, I could see, with consummate gentleness; she responded to the lightest touch. When we reached the valley floor, the track widened, and I let her move out a bit. What a fluid, ground-covering canter she had! It was easier to sit than the queen's chair that rocked back and forth on curved braces. She tossed her head and snatched again at the rope, but I held her, and she obeyed. But I felt the power in her hindquarters and the desire to run that coursed through her. I had not intended to run her at all, not the first time, but she was convincing me. Before I could do it, I had to know if she would stop. I sat up and pulled back on the rope, squeezing my leg. She came back to me at once, slowed to a trot, and stopped. But she trembled in frustration.

"Oh, good girl, my beauty, my pretty, my love. For that you shall have your gallop on the beach."

We trotted down the sea road and turned off along a woodland path that ran down to the shore. Suddenly, as the trees thinned out, the filly shied, screamed, and reared. I grabbed her mane to keep from sliding off, she whirled and tried to bolt back the way we had come, but I turned her and made her stand, facing the sea. She must never have seen the sea before! It must be as amazing to her as it was to me the first time I saw it. I stroked her neck, wet with the sweat of fear, and gradually she calmed.

I turned her away, and we rode along the dry shingle, where the sand is firm.

"All right, my lovely one, now let's see what you can do." And I gave her her head. She exploded out from under me so swiftly, I'd have fallen if I hadn't buried my hands in her whipping mane. I clung there, bent over her withers, as the ground flew by and the salt spray stung my cheeks and the west wind brought tears to my eyes. She fairly flew over the ground—I felt nothing but speed, like a spear flying. She raced past the place where Peleth always slowed down, winded, and past the last trail up from the beach. I pulled the rope in vain; when she felt the pressure, she leaned against it, increasing her speed. The trees became blurs, the sea a pounding accompaniment to her hooves. There were treacherous rocks ahead, I knew, sharp, black boulders that protruded from the soft sand like wolf's teeth—The Fangs they were called—and there was no way around them. They were a natural boundary. Fighting my panic so the mare would not sense it, I sang to her again, steadying my gulping breath, and straightened up as much as I could. Whether it was my song or the motion of my body I know not, but at last she slackened her pace, and by the time The Fangs came into view she was cantering easily, tossing her head, enjoying herself.

I brought her to a halt and turned her around. Her nostrils were flared wide, and her sides heaved, but she did not seem tired. She was not even lathered; any other horse I knew would have been dead.

"Well, my pretty one," I said, patting her neck and her rump as we started the walk back, "you are in wonderful condition. You have been loved by someone who loves horses, that is easy to see. I think I must make it a goal of mine to someday meet this knight who raised you and thank him for this gift. Yes, when Elaine goes to Caer Camel, I shall go with her, to thank him. For while you are the High King's gift, it was Lancelot who made you what you are. And I have a name for you now. I will name you Zephyr, after the west wind, for you fly as swiftly as the wind and yet are as gentle as the sea breeze. Someday I shall meet this great Sir Lancelot and thank him for my Zephyr."

6 ❀ MERLIN

Gwillim's visit was the first of many by Welsh princes. We had one or two a month, I believe, come to offer for Elaine's hand. Alyse and Pellinore were proud and happy but they were guided by Elaine's decision, and she always refused her suitors. At first she was barely polite, but as time wore on she, too, was flattered by the attention and grew condescendingly courteous. No one offered for me and in time Elaine passed from gloating into a genuine sorrow for my condition. I did not much mind the absence of suitors; my head was much too full of Zephyr to have room for men.

But Elaine's pity nearly drove me to distraction. "I am ten times the rider she is," I railed at Ailsa when we were alone, "and twice the seamstress! I can do figures in my head and read as well as anyone, and speak better Latin than most! And even though she is beautiful, she is vain about it, as if her beauty were something she had earned herself and not a gift of God! How can she be so cruel to me? In her eyes I am a poor, impoverished orphan—like Cam, the cripple—just because she has grown a bosom and I have not!"

Good Ailsa hugged me and calmed my weeping and told me, in her motherly way, that things would change as the wheel of time went round. The last would become first, she crooned, and the low made high. I frowned and looked at her askance: Where had I heard those words before?

In the month of the Raven near the autumn equinox, almost five years to the day after his victory at Caer Eden, King Arthur wed Guenwyvar of Ifray. There had been much fighting during the summer, but the High King managed to find three weeks of peace in which to marry. Then, with his bride bedded and the elders satisfied, he went back to war. His young Queen was left in

Caerleon, protected by his soldiers, with all the people daily watching her waistline to see if the High King had bred his heir in her. Elaine envied her, but I cannot say that I did.

King Arthur's victories continued, and work continued on the new fortress of Caer Camel. One Gaius Marcellus, grandson of Ambrosius' chief engineer, designed it—the fortifications, the groundwork, the buildings, and the open places. He had even given directions for the quarrying of the stone. The fortress was to be the biggest, strongest, and best defended in all the kingdoms, a gathering place for Britons, a warning to Saxons, a symbol to all of the High King's power. And after the bishop of Caerleon had blessed the cornerstone, it was whispered behind doors, Merlin the Enchanter, in a ceremony of his own, had looked into the flames, foreseen a glorious future, and sanctioned its building. After that, Arthur gave the orders to proceed.

Merlin was at Caerleon for the High King's wedding and stayed behind when Arthur and his troops rode north. He was the most trusted member of Arthur's household, and the most feared, as well. The King's sister Morgan was promised in marriage to Urien of Rheged, and since fighting in the east near Elmet required the High King's presence, Merlin was left to escort the princess and her train to Rheged for her wedding. They left on a hot day in October and traveled north through Wales.

King Pellinore and Queen Alyse had attended the High King's wedding but had not taken Elaine and me, much as we had begged to go. As a guilt gift, perhaps, they agreed to let us accompany them to meet the princess Morgan's train and pay homage to her. Elaine and I were beside ourselves with excitement. Elaine and Queen Alyse were going to ride in a litter, and they thought it only right that I should, too, but I begged and pleaded with good King Pellinore to be allowed to ride my new mare. It was not unknown for ladies, especially when young, to travel on horseback; I was sure the only reason Elaine chose the litter was because she did not have a mount as fine as mine. When she complained to her father that she had outgrown Welsh ponies he had given her Peleth, but she could barely handle him, old though he was. Pellinore at last gave in and said I could ride, but only if I rode Peleth. With tears of frustration, I begged him to allow me to ride Zephyr. He thought her too young, too flighty, but I convinced him by giving him a demonstration. In five months she had learned a lot and would do anything I asked. At the end of my demonstration, he was silent for a while, stroking her neck and looking up at me. At last he nodded.

"Use a saddle, for form's sake," was all he said.

We started out on a brilliant, crisp day, with sixty troopers in our party and twelve pack mules with all the tents, gear, and bridal gifts. I rode between King Pellinore and the litter, where he thought I was safest. In obedience to his wishes, I had on my best tunic of a dark, forest green, with a light-green mantle for warmth. I had woven threads of green and blue into Zephyr's bridle and into her braided mane. I wondered if there would be anyone in the princess' party who had known the filly. If so, I wanted to make sure a good report reached the knight who had trained her.

With the cool weather and the crowd of horses, she was very excited, and harder to sit than I expected. King Pellinore shot me a look from under his bushy brows, but I only smiled in return and quietly sang to the mare. She settled down, as I knew she would, and by midday was perfectly calm and well behaved. On the evening of the third day we reached the meeting of the roads from Caerleon and Glevum. We had been there only an hour when the royal escort came in sight. From our tent, we watched them set up camp, admiring the fine horses and trying to see if we could distinguish any of the royal party. Elaine and I shared a tent with Ailsa, Grannic, Leonora, and Cissa—we were all in a fever, as eager to catch a glimpse of Merlin the Enchanter as of the princess Morgan. But it was many hours before we were called to audience. We changed into our finest gowns and followed King Pellinore and Queen Alyse through the crowd of troopers, courtiers, and guards, to the royal tent. The servants followed, bearing our gifts.

The princess Morgan, daughter of King Uther and Ygraine his Queen, sat on a gilded chair, dressed in a heavy red gown. Her hair was dark brown and decked with a circlet of red gold; around her neck and wrists hung jewels of every color, and on her fingers she wore rings of ruby, pearl, and sapphire. She was only fifteen—she looked twenty. Her eyes were a golden brown that did not suit her coloring; she was not pretty, really, but rather proud and distant. Now she was about to wed a major king, a man with lands wider than Lot's or Pellinore's, but a man old enough to be her father. No doubt her future had been a matter of negotiation among Arthur, Urien, and Queen Ygraine. I wondered if she dreaded going to it. I shuddered involuntarily. It was not fair that happiness in a woman's life should depend so completely upon a man.

Courtiers crowded around her at a respectful distance while the servants laid our gifts at her feet, and King Pellinore performed the introductions. She smiled as Elaine made her curtsy, but at me she only stared and barely nodded. I flushed with embarrassment—it was almost a slight! What had I done?

Among the gifts we had brought, goblets and carved platters, thick warm blankets woven from good Welsh fleece, and ornaments of beaten silver from the mines near Snowdon, were several silken hangings for the new queen's chamber. Alyse and her ladies had sewn them and then we all had stitched decorative patterns in different colors of thread. One of these, of white silk with a mare's head in the center and colts frolicking in fields of green at each corner, caught her attention. She motioned for the servant to hold it up to the light.

"This one is most unusual," she said. "The stitching is very fine and the use of color shows an eye for beauty. I thank you, Queen Alyse, I shall use this for my bridal bed."

Queen Alyse curtsied low.

"Thank you, gracious Princess. But I cannot take credit for the workmanship. That silk was done by my ward, Guinevere of Northgallis."

Princess Morgan turned to stare at me, and her eyes grew cold. The smile left her lips, but her breeding held. "This is fine work indeed, for so young a maid. Thank you, Guinevere. I shall remember it."

Something moved in the darkness behind her stool—I felt eyes on me suddenly, and my flesh crept on my bones. There was a man behind her, come from nowhere it seemed, although I suppose the truth was that I simply had not noticed him before. He was tall and thin, with black hair and beard, skin as ageless as oak bark and much the same color, and black, fathomless eyes that glared at me with intense, unwavering, malignant hatred. I began to tremble violently, trapped like an insect in the web of his gaze; conversation went on around me, it seemed no one noticed. He was wrapped in a black cloak from shoulder to boot and clutched a staff in his left hand. I knew him at once. He was Merlin.

Elaine took my arm and drew me away, as Pellinore and Alyse moved off. I was shaking so hard I could barely walk and tears stung my eyes.

"Gwen! What's wrong? Why are you shaking so?"

"Why does he hate me, Elaine? What have I done?"

"Whatever are you talking about? Who hates you?"

"Merlin."

She gasped. "Merlin! How do you know? What makes you think so?"

"Didn't you see the way he looked at me?"

She stopped and stared at me, looking puzzled and a little frightened.

"Yes, I saw him," she said finally in a halting voice, "but he wasn't looking at you. He was just watching us present the gifts. He looked kindly, I thought."

Now it was my turn to stare. I thought she was teasing me at first, but then I understood her astonishment was genuine. No one, not Pellinore, Alyse, Cissa, or Leonora, had noticed anything unusual. Was it possible I had imagined it? But I knew I had not.

I kept my thoughts to myself and did not tell Ailsa. For Merlin was perhaps the most powerful man in all Britain, and an enchanter, as well. It would not do to have him as an enemy, and my dear, superstitious nurse would die a thousand deaths, yes, and clutch her amulets forever, if I shared my fears with her. I composed myself for sleep that night as usual, but sleep did not come. I lay awake, uneasy and full of fear, until the dark time at moonset. Then I seemed to feel a heaviness come upon my spirit, and I sank into sleep. Almost at once I saw Merlin's face again—not angry this time, but sorrowful. His black eyes bored through me with urgency and feeling, with beseeching, almost, but I knew not for what. I sensed longing, desperation, and then a breath, a catspaw touch of deep love. At last, his quest unsatisfied, he seemed to sigh with a sorrow from the depths of the earth. He nodded kindly, as if in benediction, and turned sadly away. As I drifted into forgetfulness, I knew even in my sleep that it was not a dream; I knew that Merlin's power had reached me where I lay, that he had seen something in me that had broken his heart and left him desolate.

In the morning, everything was packed and made ready for departure, but no one could leave until the royal party left first. I was ill with fatigue and fear and would have remained in the tent until all the farewells were said, but the tents were struck early and I had nowhere to hide. Elaine kept near Queen Alyse and Leonora, but I slipped away when no one was looking. It was very busy, with servants and soldiers bustling everywhere, everyone wanting to get an early start. I went to the horse lines and took an apple to Zephyr. She nickered a greeting and daintily took the fruit from my hand. The grooms had already saddled her, but I readjusted her saddle cloths and her girth, for I knew how she liked them best. Then I rebraided her mane, crooning to her all the while and keeping well out of sight. But I knew that I could not hide from a magician. Magic was in the air that morning, all about me, the still, awful dread I had known by the spring pool in Northgallis. I was amazed that no one else seemed to notice it. Everyone was bustling about his chores, calling out morning greetings, exchanging bawdy jokes, laughing and grunting, moving and working. Only I, it seemed, was caught in this bright web of stillness, where the very air I breathed was alive with the whisperings of phantoms.

Quite suddenly, he was beside me. I had not heard a footfall of his approach. He was plainly dressed; only the gold and red enamel Dragon brooch at his shoulder gave a clue to his identity. I believe I gasped as I sank to my curtsy.

"My lord Merlin."

He reached out and took my hands, raising me quickly. To my surprise, his flesh was warm and comforting. He did not let go of my hands, but held them in his own and looked at me with kind, deep eyes. I was shaking, and the air around me positively sang with voices, but he stilled them. I saw him do it. He gave his head a quick shake, and the world went quiet.

"Do not be afraid," he said simply.

I could not speak. Neither could I take my eyes from his face.

"Your heart's desire will be granted in six months," he said. "After that, it is with the gods. You cannot change your fate, my dear, and neither can I."

"You—you don't hate me, my lord?"

Something flashed in the eyes then, and the corners of his thin mouth moved. "For his sake, I cannot. Glory and greatness are built on love. What will be, will be. Let it be so."

He dropped my hands then, as pounding filled my ears, and he actually bowed to me before he left. The last thing I heard as the world went dark was a groom calling out in panic, "The lady Guinevere has fainted!"

King Pellinore made me ride home in the litter with Elaine, convinced I was ill. Or course I told Elaine all about it, and her eyes went wide with astonishment that Merlin the Enchanter should single me out to speak to.

"But is that all he said? What does it mean?"

"I have no idea what it means."

"But it was a blessing, wasn't it, and not a curse?"

I went cold inside at the thought. "I don't know, Elaine. Would he have held my hands while he cursed me? Would he have bowed? Why did he come to find me in the midst of the bustle of departure, just to tell me not to be afraid? How could he possibly think I would not be afraid?"

"But you are brave, Gwen. I've seen you—flying through the air with Zephyr. It makes me weak with fear to watch you!"

"Nonsense. I'm not afraid of Zephyr. I think you have to be afraid in order to be brave. And I am truly afraid of Merlin. Do you believe—a pagan enchanter has power over a Christian?" I was reminded of my conversation with Gwillim, long ago. Did he command real powers, or just my thoughts and dreams? If I did not believe he had power over me—but that was the trouble. Christian or not, I did believe it. I knew it.

"Ask Father Martin," Elaine advised. "He will know. He speaks to God."

When we were home, and I had convinced Queen Alyse that I had recovered from my faintness, I sought out Father Martin. He was a robust and comely man of about thirty who enjoyed the company of peasants and low folk as much as that of Pellinore's nobles. He was not a scholar like Iakos, but he was warm and approachable. I found him in his garden, surrounded by group of dirty, brown-skinned children in ragged clothing. They were listening open-mouthed to the story of Jonah and the Whale. I wondered if any of them were sons of fisher-folk and what would happen when they next went out upon the sea.

Father Martin rose when he saw me and smiled. The children filed out, eyes downcast, and then we heard them running down to the village, hollering and shouting, and Father Martin laughed.

"To have such energy! I would I could be young again. Well, my lady Guinevere, to what do I owe the honor of this visit?"

"I wish to know the answer to a question, Father, and I think only you can answer it."

He paused and led me to a stone bench among the pear trees. "I will certainly answer it if I can, my lady."

"Do pagan enchanters have powers over spirits, or only God?"

I don't know what he was expecting, but it wasn't that. He stared a moment and then almost smiled. "Are you referring to any pagan enchanter in particular, my lady?"

"Yes. To Merlin."

He cleared his throat then, and looked away. "Ahhh. Merlin." He studied the clouds for a while and then turned to me. "May I know what brought this on, my lady? Has something happened that concerns Merlin?"

"Y—yes, Father. I met him. He spoke to me."

"And he frightened you."

"He told me not to be afraid. But he—he did frighten me."

Father Martin took both my hands, as Merlin had done, but the effect was not the same. There was nothing in them. They were human hands.

"You know, Guinevere, that the Lord God is the True God. He loves His children, especially the innocent. He protects you, child, He protects you daily. You have nothing to fear from Merlin while God's Hand is over you."

"Then Merlin has no power? Or is it that God's is stronger?"

Father Martin looked uncomfortable. "There are many kinds of power, child. There is the kind of power the High King wields against his enemies. There is the kind of power the soothsayers and hill witches have over the minds of simple folk. But the kind of power God grants is greater than all of them. It is the power of love."

I did not understand him. "Do you class Merlin with the soothsayers, then? Does he only have power over those who believe in him? Is it so with God, also?"

Father Martin crossed himself quickly, shocked. "Hush, my sweet child, it's blasphemy to say such a thing. That God's holy power could depend on something as frail as the will of a human! No, no, never think it. No matter what you believe, my dear girl, God will love you and protect you. His love is everlasting."

"Forgive me, Father. I did not mean to blaspheme. It's only—I want to know if Merlin has power or not."

Father Martin sighed and struggled with his words. "I do not know the man myself," he said at last. "But I have heard of his many doings. I will not deny that he has power. But they say his power has always been used for the good, for building and making. It is God's power, though even Merlin may not know it."

I wanted to believe him, but I did not. Jesus had never come to me in my sleep the way that Merlin had.

"What, if I may ask, my lady, did Merlin say to you?"

Now it was my turn to look away and feel nervous. "He—he spoke of the future, I think, but it was very unclear. I mean, I didn't understand him. He said what will be, will be. He said glory and greatness are built on love. But he seemed very sorry about it. It was the way he said it. As if he could see my future and it broke his heart."

Father Martin looked relieved and a little awed. Merlin's words, even secondhand, could strike awe into the heart of a Christian priest.

"He has told you the truth about the power of love," Father

Martin said. "It is a thing a wise man knows. And if Merlin the Enchanter is concerned about your future, Lady Guinevere, it must be a mighty future indeed."

I rose. I had learned what I came to learn. Father Martin believed every word out of Merlin's mouth. He was even staring at me with wonder. I wanted to cry.

"Thank you for your time, Father Martin," I managed, gulping. "I must—I must get back. The queen—" I choked on the words and turned away.

He rose hastily. "Whatever happens, my lady, God will protect you. Do not be afraid."

I shook my head as I hurried toward the gate, brushing tears from my eyes.

Poor Father Martin tried again. "Merlin cannot hurt you, now or ever."

I turned as I opened the gate and looked up into his worried face. With an effort I found my voice, and to my surprise, it sounded calm. "Perhaps not. But he will never forgive me, either, for whatever it is I am to do."

In bed that night, I told Elaine everything that had passed. It did not surprise her that Father Martin believed in Merlin's powers. Only a fool would not believe in them, so well known were they. I was the one she found puzzling.

"But what did you expect, Gwen? You never doubted Merlin's power. You felt it yourself, you said so. So why do you think Father Martin has let you down? What does God have to do with Merlin?"

"Can Merlin see the future, Elaine? Truly, do you think he can?"

"Of course. He sees what he wills to see. If he has seen yours, you may be sure it is important somehow." She paused. "If your future is important, it must mean you will be a great lady someday. Perhaps you will follow me to the High King's court. Perhaps you will marry one of the Companions."

"Elaine, you must know by now that is not my ambition."

Elaine smiled slyly. "What about the other thing he said? What is your heart's desire, Gwen? To marry a prince?"

"No, by Mithra. Just to be a woman, like you. The older I get the less I think I ever want to be married."

Elaine was scandalized. "You can't mean you want to be a spinster! And you shouldn't swear by Mithra now that you've been baptized. Gwen, what's the matter with you? Don't you want to be a queen someday and have lands of your own?"

"They won't be lands of my own. They'll be my husband's lands. He'll want to manage them all by himself, because he's the man and I'm just the keeper of his house. He won't even discuss what's going on in the world because 'it's not a fit subject for young maids.' Whether I'm happy or not will depend completely upon him, and not at all upon me. I tell you, Elaine, I hate the thought of it."

"Well, you don't have to marry anyone like that. Mother says so. She's let me refuse all the young men, even when Father is so furious, because she says it's only right that both husband and wife should want the same thing. And she'll do the same for you. I'm sure she will."

"Oh, Elaine, do you really think she would? Even though Gwarthgydd and Pellinore might want it differently? Would she really require my consent? I tell you now, I don't think I ever want to go near Caer Camel, or see the King's Companions. Not if Merlin is nearby." And I shivered.

Elaine put her arms around me and hugged me warmly. "You will come with me. I will protect you. You are meant for someone special, that much is clear. One of the Companions, without a doubt, cousin. Perhaps that young knight with the foreign name who trained your horse. Just wait and see. You'll love it at court."

Two weeks later Merlin disappeared. Princess Morgan had married King Urien, the wedding feast had lasted a week, the guests had departed. Merlin stayed on in conference with the aging bridegroom, discussing defense strategy. Lot's queen, Morgause, Morgan's half-sister stayed on waiting for a fair wind to sail back to the Orkney Isles. While her body had grown thick with childbearing, she was still the most beautiful woman at the wedding and far outshone the bride. With her was a red-headed boy of three, Lot's firstborn son, Gawaine. She had other sons at home in Orkney; one of them, the whispers went, was older than Gawaine, "the dark prince" she had left at home, but I did not believe the talk. Lot, of all people, surely would not allow the Queen to raise her bastard side by side with his own sons. At any rate, on the day Morgause sailed for Orkney, Merlin disappeared. No one could explain it. He was gone, and he left no trace.

People laughed at first and said the King's enchanter was up to his old tricks again, but as time went on faces grew sober. Always before when Merlin disappeared in one place, he reappeared somewhere else; the people always knew the enchanter was there when Arthur wanted him. But this time even Arthur could not find him. The King's troops scoured the wood where he had vanished, visited his cold hilltop cave in south Wales, hunted around Caer Camel and anywhere else they could think of, but Merlin was not there. Winter winds closed the seas, early snows blanketed the land, covering the woodland tracks, and the search parties were called off. Now King Arthur was alone.

News came from Caerleon that the young Queen was with child of the royal heir, and bonfires were lit throughout the land in celebration. King Pellinore held a feast on All Hallow's Eve in honor of the event. Elaine was green with envy, but I told her what a dreary life it would be, married to the High King.

"You'd only be a broodmare to him," I said. "That would be your foremost duty. Bear his children as fast as you could and see that they're all sons. Forget having a companion, he would never be there. Even Alyse only sees Pellinore six months of the year, and he's a homebody compared to the High King. He must always travel about the Kingdom. You would never really know him. There wouldn't be time. You would be miserable." I succeeded only in convincing myself. I never convinced Elaine. She was completely and thoroughly in love with Arthur, and there seemed to be nothing anyone could do about it.

Then, as the first snows fell, the High Queen began to ail. All Caerleon was thrown into confusion. Priests, physicians, witches, and enchanters passed in a steady stream through the young Queen's chamber. Arthur promised gold to any who could stay her bleeding and turned no one away who offered help. King Pellinore went to court to see what he could do, but, as he told us later, there was nothing anyone could do. Neither Mithra, nor Christ, nor Bilis, Eroth, Llyr nor Lluden, nor the Great Goddess of Avalon could prevent the horror that followed. Merlin might have saved the child, it was thought, but Merlin was not there. Arthur was beside himself with grief. And that poor girl, only seventeen and still a bride, died on Arthur's birthday in desperate agony, with the High King weeping at her bedside. When it was over Arthur shut himself away and for three weeks spoke to no one. Finally his officers threatened to beat down his door. Word had reached the Saxons of the King's grief, and they were massing for an attack along the great river Thames, as far west as Amesbury. This news aroused the King, but he came out from his fastness a changed man. Gone was the gaiety and exuberance of youth; this was a man quick to anger and dangerous to cross. The Saxons retreated before his fury as before a wall of flame.

The entire Kingdom of Britain grieved with Arthur, all except

Elaine. Elaine alone was serene, at peace again. He was free once more, and she was biding her time. She tired me with her fantasies and her ambition, or perhaps it was the long, dreary winter days and nights within the castle that tired me. When the midwinter thaw finally came, I spent all the daylight hours out riding. It felt so wonderful to be free again! I pitied the High King, if he could not find joy in the freedom of a horse.

One clear, bright January morning I rose early, slipped into my doeskin leggings and a warm cloak, and took Zephyr down to the shore. Her favorite run was along the beach, and afterward she was relaxed and ready for practice jumping fences. Her prowess amazed me; she could fly over any obstacle I put before her with plenty of room to spare, and she seemed to love it. She was eager that morning, tossing her head and snatching playfully at the bit, urging me to hurry. But she came back to my hand the instant I asked her and obediently walked down the track to the sea. It was a fine morning, cold and clear, the last traces of dawn painted pink streaks on the gray sea. I caressed the mare, who trembled in anticipation, and, hooking a fist in her mane, gave her her head. She shot forward, and the shore sped past in a blur. I loosened my hair with my free hand and let it whip in the wind. I felt free of everything then—the Kingdom with its constant wars, Wales with its jealous lords, and castle routine with daily lessons and strictures—all were left behind me at that moment. I was as free as the seabirds, and as wild. The future lay before me, unknown and therefore bright and beckoning. As icy air filled my lungs, I shouted aloud with joy. Zephyr responded by quickening her thundering pace, and we flew up the beach, only slowing when The Fangs came into view. As we turned and trotted back, I hugged the mare in exhilaration.

"Oh, my proud beauty, what happiness you bring me! I shall never part with you, my Zephyr. We shall always ride together!"

She nodded her head exactly as if she understood, and we cantered slowly back the way we had come. I headed her toward a track that left the beach toward the jumping field, when suddenly she started, shying violently, and almost threw me. I grabbed her mane, and only just kept her from whirling and bolting. She was shaking like a leaf in an autumn storm, and though I sang and spoke to her, she did not settle.

"What is it, my beauty? What have you sensed?"

The beach was deserted, the sea quiet. I saw no movement anywhere. But the mare was frantic and would not advance. I slid off her back and held her head close to my body. When I wrapped her nostrils in my cloak, she calmed a little, and I knew then it was something she had smelled. The light land breeze still blew at that hour, so I looked inland, up the track, searching the sparse gorse bushes that grew in the sand, toward the line of bare hardwoods that marked the edge of the woods. And I saw something. Underneath our own footprints the sand had been disturbed. It looked like something heavy had been dragged up the track, and something small and white fluttered ahead under the bushes, just short of the trees.

"Come on, my sweet, let's find out what it is." Frightened as she was, the filly followed me up the track, but as we neared the trees she snorted once and screamed. A low moan answered from the bushes, and to my amazement, the filly blew once and was quiet. The mystery was solved for her: it was human, and therefore a friend. I tied her to a sapling and left her standing peacefully while I went to see who lay half concealed and moaning in the sand.

He was a stranger. There was dark blood caked in his bright hair, and his left leg was bent at an unnatural angle. His tunic was torn, but the cloth was fine. I saw no cloak anywhere. His face was blue with cold and pain, and his eyes were closed. I drew off my cloak and covered him. He shivered violently. I laid a hand to his forehead. He was very cold. The light touch seemed to revive him, for his eyes fluttered open and he looked right at me. His eyes were a brilliant green in color, with honey-colored flecks around their dark centers; I found it impossible to look away as he stared at me.

"Forgive me my sins," he mumbled, and then he sank into unconsciousness.

I ran to the filly, beginning to shiver myself, and jumped on her back. His speech had been in Latin, but his accent was foreign. I was sure he was not Welsh, perhaps not even British. He lay on the sand by the Irish Sea. My heart pounded in time with the filly's galloping strides as we raced back to the castle. Was he one of the Irish devils all good Welsh children had been taught to fear?

I roused the castle with the news, and King Pellinore sent troops with a litter down to fetch the stranger, but he would not let me show them the way. He ordered the grooms to care for Zephyr, and he roused Leonora, who took one look at me and threw me into a hot bath. Queen Alyse scolded me for parting with my cloak and made me go back to bed with hot bricks at my feet. I was furious with frustration, for I felt perfectly fine, only cold, and I wanted news of the stranger.

Thank goodness Elaine was adept at eavesdropping, for she tripped in and out of my room all day with whatever news she picked up. When they found the stranger he was delirious and half dead with cold. He was not expected to live, so they did not put him in the dungeon, but in a guest chamber near the guard tower. They bathed him and placed hot bricks wrapped in herb-soaked towels around his body. King Pellinore's physician set his leg and bandaged his head, and Father Martin gave him the last rites, for it was clear he was a Christian. In his delirium he called upon the Christian God and his angels to save him. But most of the time he rambled in a tongue no one could understand.

By nightfall he was hot with fever and still delirious. An Irish kitchen slave, captured in a thwarted raid upon our shores eight years before, was brought into the room to see if he could understand the stranger's delirious speech. The man broke into tears at hearing once more the lilting Gaelic of his homeland.

"And so," Elaine announced, perched on my coverlet, "he is Irish, just as you thought, Gwen. If he lives he will be a prisoner, and if he is a lord of some kind, a hostage, which could bring Father some Irish gold. They say he is young, not over twenty. What does he look like?"

I saw again the white, drawn face with the matted gold hair and the mesmerizing eyes. "He's the handsomest man I've ever seen."

Elaine giggled. "You'd better not fall in love with an Irish prince, Gwen. I don't think Mother would let you go to Ireland for all the gold in Rome. She saw his clothes, you know, and said they were of good quality. So he might be someone important. Isn't it exciting?"

"But how did he come to be lying on our beach?"

"I don't know yet. But I'll know before dinner is over."

I was not allowed up for dinner, but Ailsa brought me a meal in bed and fixed me a hot posset. I did not protest this care, for my throat was beginning to feel raw, and I knew I would be abed for two days with the usual winter chills. But Elaine was as good as her word and had all the news by bedtime.

"There was a raid last night," she confided, eyes shining. "The thaw has opened the seas, and Father has had the beach patrolled for the last five days. Last night a ship was sighted, and four boatloads of ruffians came ashore, led by a young hothead, or so the soldiers say. They didn't get far, and most of them escaped back to their ship, but the fighting was fierce, and many were wounded.

The soldiers rounded them up and they're in the dungeon now, but I guess they missed this one. I wonder if he's the leader."

"From your description of the raid, he can't be much of a leader."

Elaine laughed. "Well, he's no Arthur. But the Irish aren't thinking fighters. They never have been. They fight from passion. Show them cold steel, and they turn and flee."

I grinned at her. "If he lives, I'll be sure to let our stranger know your good opinion of him."

"I don't care what he thinks of me," she retorted. "He will always be an Irishman, and I'm going to be a British queen."

At least, I thought later, as I drew the covers around me and fell towards sleep, she didn't say "Queen of Britain."

7 ✿ FION

I lay abed a week with fever and chills. I was nursed and cosseted, but given no news and forbidden to ask questions. An air of secrecy seemed to envelop the castle. Elaine was with me often, but turned the conversation from any topic of interest except King Arthur and his doings. He was doing much, it seemed, even in the winter snows. Tales of courageous deeds and of murderous rages were told and retold; he was no longer referred to as a youth. He was nineteen now and a man. Wherever he raised Excalibur in the defense of Britain he was victorious. Ten major battles and thousands of skirmishes lay behind him; he had never received so much as a scratch from a Saxon weapon. Yet in the midst of his glory he grieved, for his lost wife, his lost child, and his lost friend, the great enchanter. His tread was heavier; his smiles were rarer. He got on with the business of defeating his enemies and unifying the kingdoms with a cold determination that made his own men afraid of him.

Of the Irish stranger, Elaine would say nothing except that he still lived. But her eyes sparkled, and she winked at me when Ailsa or Grannic's back was turned. Finally my strength returned, and I grew weary of convalescence. I insisted on getting up to sit by the fire, or taking short walks on Ailsa's arm. When after two weeks I was fully recovered, the wild winter weather set in, and we were snowbound. I couldn't even get to the barn to visit Zephyr. I had to spend my days with the rest of the women in the weaving room, spinning, weaving, sewing, talking. We joined the men at meals in the dining hall, but otherwise we were cloistered together. It was the dreadful winter routine. People got fractious without exercise in the sun, and personalities began to rub one another into irritation. All this I knew and expected, but this winter was better than most. The Queen's ladies were often in buoyant spirits, teasing each other and laughing, singing new songs, even weaving new patterns—and all because of our stranger.

His name was Fion. He was, it seemed, quite a catch. He was certainly an Irish prince, and if the kitchen slave who served as translator was to be believed, he was *the* Prince of Ireland, son of Gilomar the King. He had lived through a three-day fever, survived two leechings and the setting of his leg, and was fast recovering from a chest cold. He ate like a young wolf and sang like a bard. He had already picked up enough Welsh to carry on a conversation, and he flirted with the ladies, even Queen Alyse, from dawn until dusk. He showed no fear and bore no grudge against his captors. He was a hostage, and he knew it. But he appeared to be in no hurry to return to his native land. As long as there was a woman in his room, he spouted poetry, sang songs, teased, admired, cajoled, and flirted. He had captivated every woman in the palace, from queen to cook, and although he was rapidly recovering his health, there was no talk of moving him into the dungeon with his fellows. The queen's ladies waited upon him themselves. King Pellinore seemed glad they had the diversion; everyone was in a better temper.

"Saints be praised," Cissa said as she sat spinning, "if the rascal didn't pinch me again this morning! And me old enough to be his mother!"

"He's a handsome rascal, to be sure," Leonora added. "And an amorous young devil. Do they breed them so in Ireland on purpose, to conquer our hearts?"

Queen Alyse laughed. "If he is on a mission to subdue Wales by winning its women, he is very likely to succeed. I have seen the way he looks at my daughter when he thinks I do not observe him."

Elaine blushed and I grinned. So this was what she had been hiding from me! She had an admirer, and this one, it seemed, she did not object to.

"Mother, please," Elaine protested. "He's a hooligan. A foreigner."

"Well, my dear," Alyse said smoothly as she bent over her stitching, "Welsh princesses have married foreigners before now. To be Queen of Ireland would be a great honor, would it not?"

I glanced quickly at Elaine. It was written on her face as clearly as the writing on any scroll that she wished only to be Queen of Britain.

"Mother!" Elaine cried. "I am British! I will never leave my homeland! I would rather be a British spinster than an Irish queen!"

All the ladies laughed and nodded approvingly, and I saw it had just been a leg-pull. Alyse had been teasing—indeed, I thought, she would be the last one to want to send her daughter across the sea where she might never see her again.

"Such poetry!" Cissa exclaimed. "And such good Latin he speaks. He's an educated man, you may be sure of it. This morning when I brought him his willow tea, he was on about the angel again."

"The Angel from Heaven who feeds his soul?" Leonora asked. "He is on about her day and night. You would think a man lying half frozen on a winter beach would see devils and monsters, not angels. He has a vivid imagination."

"What is this about angels?" I asked. "I have not heard this story before. Is it an Irish tale?"

"No, my lady. The young man had a dream as he lay upon the shore. He claims he saw an Angel of God, a vision of loveliness with hair of white fire, who touched him just as life was about to expire and brought him back from the jaws of death." She smiled benevolently as my heart began to sink. "He claims he saw a halo of light around her head, the stars of Heaven in her eyes, and the joy of everlasting life in her smile. Oh, he has a way with words, that one. He had Cissa and me believing him, he did."

Elaine looked at me suddenly and made a face. "He's probably talking about Gwen. He's just dressing it up. After all, she saved him."

"Yes, and in addition to all our thanks, Prince Fion would like to thank you Guinevere when you have regained your strength," Alyse said. "But I warn you, he thinks we are playing upon his credulity. He does not believe a child could save his life. And he certainly does not believe any king or queen in their right minds would allow a ward of such tender years to venture forth alone on a frosty winter morning along a beach where raiders had been slain the night before."

It was meant as a rebuke, so I bowed my head and said nothing, but I resented it. How was I to know there had been a raid? They told us nothing, because we were young maids. If the weather had been warm, Elaine and I would have sneaked up to the tower wall and learned of the news ourselves, but I did not see how I was to be held responsible for my ignorance as things were. One thing was clear—gone was my freedom with Zephyr.

When Elaine and I went up to our room to change for dinner,

we walked in silence. I was hurt that Queen Alyse had referred to me as a child, and here I was only three months short of fourteen. It was the old wound again, and sore still from constant bruising. It was not until we were in our chamber and half undressed that Elaine spoke to me.

"Gwen, if you take him from me, I will never forgive you."

I simply stared at her. "What on earth are you talking about?"

"Mother will take you to see Fion, and once he looks at you he will never again look at me."

"Oh, please be sensible, Elaine. Do not start this again. You are Pellinore's daughter. You're a woman, and I'm a child. Your own mother said so."

Elaine was smiling, but her eyes were unhappy. "Mother hasn't seen you in your undergarments recently." She came up to me; she was a full head shorter. "Your shape is changing. Didn't you even know it?"

She led me to the polished bronze we kept by the window, and I looked at my reflection in some astonishment. I had not known it. I had not felt it. But there it was. My breasts were swelling, and my waist looked smaller because my hips, always as narrow as a boy's, were widening ever so slightly. At last I looked like a young girl on the verge of womanhood, the way Elaine had looked at ten.

"Elaine!" I cried, and hugged her, as the tears streamed down my cheeks. "Oh, Elaine, perhaps old Merlin was right, God rest his soul. Perhaps I shall be a woman at last!"

Elaine did not return my embrace.

"You will be too beautiful to bear when it happens," she said slowly. "I know already what will happen. Every man who looks at you will love you."

"Nonsense," I said, taking her hand. "You underestimate yourself. You are pretty, Elaine, and are the king's daughter. I am an orphan. Anyway, I don't want Fion. You don't, either, if it comes to that. Why should it matter what he thinks?"

Elaine would not look at me. "I'm not talking just about Fion."

But I did not understand her. "Come, I will guarantee you that after I have met him, his admiration for you will be undiminished. Shall we place a wager on it?"

"I am not such a fool as that."

Her good humor had vanished, but mine simply grew and expanded like a giant bubble, filling all the space between us and gradually, as it enveloped her, she acquiesced to its power and joined me, at least outwardly, in my happiness.

I did not forget Merlin the Enchanter in my prayers that night. Whether he was alive or dead, I prayed to God to be merciful to him, to save his soul, for what he had foretold was coming to pass, and in three swift months I should have my heart's desire.

"Come, Guinevere, and bring the basket of new bread." Obediently I fell into the train of waiting women burdened with clean linens, fine silks, and bowls of dried fruit and nuts, who followed Queen Alyse up the staircase to the prisoner's chambers.

The guard at the door smiled and shook his head when he saw us and, bowing to Queen Alyse, let us pass.

The chamber was large, with a narrow window facing the sea, and a log fire burning merrily in the grate. Fion sat on the window seat, bathed and dressed in a fine linen shirt, loose leather leggings, and wrapped in a warm, russet cloak. His splinted leg he held straight before him, and as we entered he rose, leaning on a stout staff.

"Welcome, my fair ladies, my morning nymphs." He spoke Welsh with a charming lilt to his voice and put a softness to the rough word-sounds that was foreign, and yet pleasing, to our ears. He was tall and handsome, standing there in his dark cloak with his bright hair falling across his brilliant eyes. He made me want to smile, and my heart beat faster. I pulled the hood of my cloak around my face and turned away with the others to place my basket upon the table. Queen Alyse was greeting him formally, as her husband's prisoner, but she used the tone of voice she might have used for a son. One by one the waiting women curtsied to him and left, until only Leonora and I remained. Queen Alyse signaled me to come forward, and as I rose from my curtsy my hood fell back, and I looked up into his eyes.

He gasped and fell back on the window seat, wincing with pain.

"Dear Lord in Heaven!" he cried in Latin. "Angel of God! 'Tis thee in the flesh! O Lord, have mercy upon my soul!" And he crossed himself reverently.

"My dear prince Fion," Alyse began smoothly, "may I present my ward, my sister's daughter Guinevere of Northgallis. Guinevere, Prince Fion, son of Gilomar of Ireland."

I smiled at him and extended my hand. He took it between both of his and gazed into my face. Finally, as the silence began to be awkward, he spoke in Welsh. "You are real, my lady? You are flesh and blood, as I am? May the blessed saints be praised! An Angel of God and real to the touch." He lifted my hand to his lips, and from the corner of my eye I saw the queen's eyebrows rise.

"It was Guinevere," she said, "who found you on the beach and sent my husband's troops to find you. It is she you must thank for your life."

Fion turned to her in amazement. "My beautiful Alyse, I thought you said a child had found me." And his brilliant eyes traveled from my face slowly down my gown and back up again, while I turned scarlet, and he held my hand firmly in his own.

Queen Alyse smiled. "She is at an age when every day makes a difference in a maid. It seems I have not been paying close enough attention."

She turned away, and I hastily withdrew my hand and followed, but at the door she stopped.

"Leonora," she said, "stay with the lady Guinevere awhile. I am sure our foreign prince would like to ease his conscience and thank her for the gift of life. Come to me in an hour." And she left us there.

I was dumbfounded. Leonora, with a secret smile, settled herself before the fire and began stitching a silk shirt, no doubt for Fion. I whirled around. The Irishman had risen, clutching his staff, and held out his hand to me. It was all too, too clear. He was not good enough for Elaine, of course. The mother's ambition lagged not far behind the daughter's. But he was perfect for me. She had waited until I had my health and color back before she brought me to him, for *his* sake, not for mine. By leaving us alone with only Leonora for chaperone, she was giving her consent to his courtship as clearly as if she had spoken it aloud. Alyse was no fool. It would suit her purposes very well to see me married and settled in Ireland. Pellinore would have friends across the Irish Sea, and they could stop worrying that I would somehow cast a shadow across Elaine's future.

Poor Fion seemed unaware of all that had passed. He simply stared at me with his glorious eyes and blessed aloud the luck that had brought him to Wales. I walked demurely to the settle on the other side of the fire and took up some embroidery.

"We are pleased to see you looking so well, Prince Fion," I said, in just the tone Alyse had used. "Our clean Welsh air seems to do you good."

He hobbled over to the hearth and stood with his back to the fire, looking from one of us to the other.

"The air here is very fine indeed, my lady. And I have been nursed by the loveliest gentlewomen in all Britain, I am sure.

How could I not return swiftly to health under such care?" His tone was very cool. I glanced up. His face, before so expressive, was masked like a courtier's, and he nodded gravely to me. "I would know, if my lady would not think it impertinent of a stranger, and a hostage one at that, where Northgallis is? And what fortunate king names you as his daughter?"

I put down my needlework and looked up at him. "Sir, I am an orphan. My mother died at my birth. My father was King Leodegrance of Northgallis, who sent me here to live with my kin before he died. Northgallis lies a day's hard ride eastward, a small kingdom in North Wales."

He smiled gently. "My sympathies for such misfortune. And I? Do you wish to know what manner of hooligan, as I think you Welsh call it, you have in your midst?"

I smiled back. "If you are a hooligan, my lord, at least you are an educated one, a Christian one, and at the moment, a tamed one."

He grinned, and his face lit. Leonora raised an eyebrow.

"Indeed," he replied. "Tamed and caged. And completely at your service, Guinevere of Northgallis." He bowed deeply and made it look graceful, although it was obviously difficult with his splinted leg and staff. "If my good Leonora will permit me to sit at her side?" He made an obeisance to Leonora, who blushed and hastily made room for him on the bench.

"You don't fool me, my young lord. You sit here not for my company, but so you may better see young Guinevere."

He laughed and kissed her cheek quickly. "And could you blame me now? Is there a lass in all the Northern Isles to match her? Would she not grace any king's hall?"

I bowed my head as he jabbered on and picked up my stitching. But I noted that his position on the bench enabled him to stretch his injured leg out straight upon it, and this seemed to afford him some relief. It had not occurred to me before, but he must have been all the time in some pain. I decided to be direct.

"And now, Fion, son of Gilomar. What manner of man are you? Did I do my foster father a disservice by bringing you into our midst? You came to raid us—are you now a spy?"

He looked up swiftly and with new interest. "I have been here three weeks. You are the first person to ask me a serious question." He paused. "My father calls himself King of Ireland. But if you know aught of Ireland you know we have ten or twenty such kings with ten or twenty such claims. We are a proud race and like not to bend the knee. Thus we waste our strength in petty quarrels and cannot unite. The rest of the known world thinks of us only as pirates." He paused, and I struggled to keep the truth of his statement from showing on my face. "I am Gilomar's youngest son, and the last living. All my brothers were hotheads, like my father, who threw themselves at the first foe they could find. When my father was my age, and the great Ambrosius lay dying, Merlinus came to Ireland to find the standing stones to bedeck his grave. He was protected by a small force led by Uther Pendragon. My father had five hundred men at his back, but it took Uther only three hours to repel his attack and send him fleeing. You have not heard this story? It is true. I tell it to illustrate the great difference between you British and we Irish. My father has not changed. My brothers were just like him. I am not. When my father insisted that I show my mettle and lead a raid upon your shores, I resolved to do it for one reason only. I wanted to see Britain. I want to meet this son of Uther's who knows how to rule men. Whether I go as a hostage or as a free man, I wish to see Arthur Pendragon and judge him for myself." He was looking into the fire as he spoke, and the passion of his feeling gave strength to his face. "If he is a true man, I will pledge my allegiance to him. And then perhaps in time my Ireland may become part of the civilized world."

In the silence the snapping of the burning logs was the only sound. I was moved. He had dealt straight with me and had spoken to me as if I were his peer. "I am sure you will get your wish, my lord."

He slowly came out of his deep thoughts and smiled again. "That's as may be. Being a hostage can be chancy. You must stay on the good side of your host and not wear out your hospitality. Pray let me recite you a poem from one of our famous bards."

He regaled us for a long time. He had a lovely speaking voice and an accurate memory. Leonora warmed willow bark tea for us at the hearth, and we all partook of the fruit we had brought him. At length he touched Leonora's arm.

"Your hour is up, good Leonora, and your duty done. Take the queen's ward away and the light out of my life."

Leonora did not know what to say. "Good sir, I beg your pardon. We may stay as long as we will, I am sure, unless we tire you."

"Heard you not the queen's orders? They struck fire in my young princess. I have no wish to force myself upon you longer than I must. You are free to go."

Leonora turned to me beseechingly.

"Fion." I rose. "It is true I was angry. But I am no longer. Time passes quickly with you, and I was pleased. If this is to be daily repeated—" I glanced at Leonora, who nodded, "—then I pray you will not dread it on my account, for I assure you that I am content to be here. That is—" I fumbled suddenly and looked away from him, "—that is, if you understand."

"I understand, Guinevere." His voice was very gentle as he slipped into Latin. "Thou art not for me."

I looked up at him gratefully and was surprised to catch him gazing at me with longing. To cover, he added hastily, "Please, my lady, if there are any books in the place, bring them that I may read aloud to you."

"I'll bring them and read them aloud to you, Prince Fion."

He stared in amazement. "What! You know your letters? Can you write, as well?" He came close to me then, his back to Leonora and grasped my hands. "For whom are you being groomed?" he demanded softly.

My bewilderment must have shown, for he released me at once and stepped back.

"Queen Alyse believes all young ladies of breeding should know reading and writing," Leonora stated, bundling up her needlework. "The lady Elaine and Guinevere have studied with a Greek scholar right along with Pellinore's sons. Someday they will make good wives to the High King's Companions, if God wills."

Fion looked thoughtful. "I see," he said. "Perhaps."

He kissed my hand before we left and begged me to give his love, his undying devotion, and his limitless admiration to the lady Elaine.

"Be sure you bring her tomorrow," he whispered. "The apple-cart must not be upset."

It occurred to me, as I followed Leonora down the hall, that in three weeks he had learned a great deal more about us than we had learned about him.

I went daily to see him at the queen's direction, and as often as she could manage it, Elaine accompanied me. She was determined to come every day, but Alyse preferred that the prince spend as much time alone with me as propriety would allow. I did not mind, for Fion and I were friends, and if Leonora chose to take our conversations as flirting and report to the queen that everything was progressing nicely, no harm was done. But Elaine could hardly bear it and was always cross when she was kept from him.

She dared not face her mother with her displeasure, so instead she grew angry and sullen with me. At bedtime, when we used to share our thoughts and hopes and secrets, she either berated me for my brazen attempts to attach Fion or refused to speak to me altogether.

"Who do you think you are?" she would snap as Ailsa brushed out my hair. "What right have you to take up all his time? He must be sick to death of all your pestering!"

"Elaine, you know perfectly well it is your own mother who commands it—"

"Fah! Don't give me that! You're disobedient enough whenever it suits you! Who went riding on the beach the morning after the raid, against orders? Who—"

"How was I to know there had been a raid on the beach? No one—"

"You're a guest in this house, Gwen, don't forget it! You can tell her no, you can feign illness, you can insult Fion, you can do a thousand things to prevent it!"

In the end, I had to apologize for my forwardness, for there was no winning an argument with Elaine. But apologies did little to improve her temper. The only time she was happy was when she went to see Fion.

Usually when Elaine was with us, Fion asked for the Story of Arthur, because she told it with such feeling. This was not a tale they told in Ireland, I suppose for obvious reasons, although they tell it now. He got the tale by heart, then retold it to us one day, with some embellishments of his own. I thought it well done, but Elaine was shocked.

"But, Fion, it is a true tale. The bits you have added are make-believe, of course, and you mustn't do it. The tale is true."

Fion looked amused. "Indeed? Dragons flying over Tintagel, King Uther changed by magic arts into the very Duke Gorolis? The prince hidden in the Enchanted Isles?" Elaine nodded, and he turned to me. "Do you believe this, Guinevere?"

It was awkward, for I had not expressed doubts about Arthur to Elaine for a long time, and I did not wish to arouse her temper, but I told Fion the truth. "It is a manner of speaking, my lord. I believe it was Merlin's plan and that he disguised King Uther and the disguise worked. I believe he protected Prince Arthur throughout his youth, and no one knows where, so one tale will do as well as another."

Fion nodded. "And that while Merlin may be a wise man, he is not—"

"Sir, make no mistake about Merlin." I met his eyes squarely. "He is an enchanter of the first order. He has power. Believe the tales you hear of Prince Merlin."

Fion's eyes widened. "*You* believe, my lady?"

Elaine jumped to my defense. "She knows it for a fact. Prince Merlin singled her out to speak to."

Fion looked thoughtful. "Did he indeed? And what did he say, if I am permitted to ask?"

"Why, nothing much," I replied, suddenly flustered because he was so intent. "He spoke about the future, but he didn't say anything specific. He told me not to be afraid."

"And right after that he disappeared," Elaine continued, "and no one has seen him since. Not even the High King. And although King Arthur has needed him desperately, he has not returned. Why, even the Saxons know and have attacked all winter, thinking King Arthur vulnerable without him, but—"

But Fion was hardly listening. He leaned upon his staff and stared thoughtfully into the fire. Elaine ended with the most recent account of Arthur's victory and of his decisive revenge. She spoke of him proudly, as if he were already her husband. I blushed for her boldness, and I thought Fion noticed it, too. He turned to her.

"And what does this prove, my pretty Elaine? Either that Merlin's magic is working still, or that he is a very wise man."

She misunderstood and tossed her head impatiently. "It proves King Arthur does not need a magician at his back to win battles or hold power."

"Precisely," Fion agreed, smiling benevolently. "He is a man now. And would the world ever have known that, had not Merlin disappeared?"

Elaine looked puzzled. Fion turned to me. "What say you, Guinevere?"

"It is true. Whether it is magic or wisdom, I know not, but I believe that Merlin's disappearance at least in this respect, has done the Kingdom good."

"Ah. Well, you might be right. This confirms me in my desire to meet the High King. Tell me, how old is he?"

"Nineteen last Christmas Eve," Elaine supplied. Fion looked shocked.

"Nineteen! I am twenty myself!" He laughed then, at himself, and shook his head. "He has led a Kingdom for six years already, and what have I done? Studied poetry and music until my father threatened to disown me, and got myself shipwrecked upon Arthur's coast."

"Pellinore's coast," Elaine corrected. Again Fion looked surprised.

"And is not Pellinore Arthur's servant? Is this Britain or Wales? You surprise me, my lady. I thought Britain was a Kingdom and a civilized land."

Elaine squirmed, aware she had erred, but not caring to demote her father.

"It is both," I replied. "This is Wales, part of Britain. These are Pellinore's ancestral lands, but he holds them for Arthur. You may ask him yourself."

Fion smiled and bowed to me. "You are a born diplomat, my lady. I knew I was in a civilized land. I must meet your King."

Elaine glanced at Leonora, who was fast asleep and snoring gently, lulled by the heat of the fire. "You may as soon as you are ransomed, whenever that will be," she said softly, tilting her head and looking coyly up at him. "But perhaps there is a quicker way."

Fion grinned. "I'm much too well bred to escape."

I giggled, but Elaine ignored me. "Offer for the hand of a maiden. If she is highborn, Pellinore must free you to avoid dishonor, and he must have the High King's consent, seeing who you are, I think."

Fion stood quite still, looking at neither of us. I glared at Elaine. How bold! How foolishly direct! It was clear she referred to herself, although she did not want him for a husband. And I knew from the careful way he guarded his expression that he was thinking of me, not of her. Merlin's words came back to me: "What will be, will be." Would it be so bad to have this handsome prince for a husband, even if it were in Ireland? He was amusing, educated, and he spoke to me about important matters, and he valued the things I valued. I could do much worse very easily. Perhaps this was my future. I did not mind. But I knew, as Fion turned toward me with a grave tenderness on his face and desire in his luminous eyes, that I did not love him.

"Perhaps," Fion said softly, "you have hit upon the solution, Lady Elaine."

Elaine flushed angrily, watching his face. Her ruse had backfired; against her will she had played into her mother's hands. A knock came at the door, and Cissa stuck her head in.

"Lady Elaine, the queen your mother requires your presence in the weaving room."

"Leave me, Cissa!" Elaine retorted. "I am not at leisure!"

"Nonsense, you know very well I'd never take such a message

to your mother. You're doing naught but flirting with Prince Fion, and that can certainly wait until later. Come, my lady, she dislikes to be kept waiting."

Elaine shrugged gracelessly. Her manners always left her when she was out of temper. She stalked past Cissa, who leaned toward me with a sly wink and whispered, "The queen's orders, my lady, to stay with the prince awhile. No need to wake up Leonora." She closed the door firmly behind her.

I studied the floor tiles carefully, my heart pounding fearfully as Fion stepped close to me. He placed his hand on my waist and drew me closer. "Guinevere, look at me." Obediently I raised my face to him, and he kissed me. Then he sighed most dolefully and backed away.

"Fion, I cannot marry you—"

"I know."

I was about to finish "because I am not yet a woman" but stopped in midbreath, astonished.

He smiled a thin, bitter smile. "I would fall to one knee if I were able, Guinevere, and beg your forgiveness for my forwardness. But, you see, I love you. I thought if I did not kiss you, I would perish of the desire." He motioned me to sit, and I collapsed gratefully into the chair. My knees were jelly. Leonora was still asleep.

"I am not a fool," he said after a long silence. "I can see your future plain enough, even if you cannot. Queen Alyse sees it, too, you know. That's why she throws you to me every day, hoping my hothead heritage will overcome my civilized veneer, and I will take you, willingly or not—"

"No!" I gasped. "She would not!"

"And then," he continued, "you would be forced to come to Ireland. And you are mistaken about the queen. She would. Do you think she would entrust her precious daughter to a chaperone who sleeps? Whenever Elaine is alone with me, there are three of them, at least."

I buried my face in my hands. "What are you talking about, Fion? You sound like Merlin, so sure and so garbled. What do you see for me? Why should they fear me so?"

"Ah. Merlin. It takes no magician's eyes to see your promise, Guinevere." He took my hand and raised me, walking me to the door. "You will come to fame and glory, as surely as the stars wheel about the heavens. In two years' time—well, I only hope I shall see it." He kissed my hand and pressed it to his cheek. "Come again tomorrow. Can you sing? Let me teach you a song.

And now leave me here with Leonora and let me spin her a yarn when she awakes."

I left him, but so troubled that I slept not at all that night, and felt ill the next day. And although my illness kept me from him, Elaine did not speak to me for almost a week. Finally I tired of her sulks and faced her. "Elaine, for heaven's sake, try to remember who you are. This behavior becomes a scullery drudge better than Pellinore's daughter."

"How dare you speak to me so!" she retorted. "You forget yourself! Your father was naught but a petty lord, a black Celt whose forefathers were hill men!"

I gasped. "How dare you insult my father! He was wise and brave and kind-hearted, and besides, there's not a Celt in Wales, including Pellinore, who is not descended from the Ancients, and you are a pin-headed hussy to think otherwise!"

Elaine screamed in fury and stamped her foot. "Stop this instant! I forbid you to speak to me ever again! I hate you, Gwen! I wish—I wish—Oh! How I wish you were ugly!" She burst into tears and threw herself upon the bed. I stood silent, stunned into speechlessness by her unexpected words.

"But, Elaine," I ventured lamely, "this is foolishness. I do not want Fion. And he does not want me. Why do you fear me so?"

"He does! He does!" She sobbed into her pillows. "It's plain as day—if you take him from me, I will kill you—I will have you turned out—sent back to your black brothers—I will—" She blubbered on unintelligibly and her distress confused me. Fighting anger, I stood looking down at her shaking body.

"Do you want him? Truly? To marry? Come, Elaine, control yourself just for the smallest second. Tell me your heart. Is Queen of Ireland your ambition?"

But she did not answer and shrugged away my hand. She did not want him. All she wanted was his admiration. Her weeping was hideous, and she did not strive to control it. Grannic hurried in, clucking and fussing, with Ailsa behind her.

"Oh, Lady Guinevere, what have you done to distress her so? Oh, dear, the poor child! Come, Ailsa, help me with her. Oh, dear!"

"Poor child indeed." I snorted in contempt. "She loves weeping better than sense, that's all."

"Guinevere!"

"I will not take insults from her any longer!"

"The lady Elaine would not insult you," Grannic protested, stroking Elaine's hair with tenderness.

"Of course not," I said bitterly. "Within the hour she will have you all believing it was *I* who insulted *her*. I don't care. Elaine, you are an ass."

"Guinevere!" they shrieked, as Elaine howled in rage, but I had already closed the door behind me.

Eventually we were made to apologize to one another, and at length we were allowed to return to Fion, but he must have guessed the trouble, for he never spoke personally to me again. When he discovered I could sing, he was delighted and taught me songs and ballads, sang with me, or just sat by the window, looking out at the Irish Sea and listening as I sang to him. And I sang to him often, to spite Elaine, who had not the voice for it.

So winter passed, and the spring rains came and washed the woods of snow. Messengers arrived from Ireland demanding ransom for the prince, and negotiations took place, week upon week, while the sun warmed the earth into bud and green grass sprang from the mud. Zephyr and I went out daily, but the beach was forbidden us now. Queen Alyse, thinking Fion's courtship progressed nicely, was graciousness itself toward me. She reminded me of a cat preening. Elaine could be no more than civil, but she was pleased that he no longer singled me out for his admiration.

Of the High King we heard only that he still grieved for his lost queen and that he still grieved for Merlin. The anguish of his grief had settled into a kind of grim despair, which worried his Companions. But his judgment of men, his justice, and his prowess as a warrior never faltered. The building on Caer Camel was nearly finished, and he planned to take possession of the fortress by midsummer. But the Saxons would not give him rest. Every time a leader fell, a younger, more eager, more bloodthirsty one rose to take his place, and the attacks continued.

A royal messenger arrived near the end of April. There were Angles and Saxons in the Caledonian Forest. Lot was marching to hem them in from the north; King Arthur was riding north and would pass through Wales in two days. Pellinore was summoned to gather troops and join him.

Negotiations for the return of Fion were nearly completed. It was time, Alyse said, he made his move.

We feasted the royal courier that night at the round table, and Elaine and I were allowed to stay and listen as the men talked about the wars. King Pellinore seemed delighted to be escaping the confines of the castle and taking to horse. He spoke eagerly of the upcoming action, and also of the Irish gold he expected to help finance the expedition. This was the first the courier had heard of an Irish prisoner, and he listened attentively as Pellinore told the story of his capture and convalescence. Of course Pellinore left women out of the story and, in so doing, missed most of what had actually happened. Elaine and I kept our faces straight, but her eyes were bright with merriment.

At the end of the story, the king's chamberlain approached and announced that the hostage, Prince Fion, begged audience of the king in the presence of the royal messenger. Pellinore was surprised and looked over at Alyse for advice. She nodded complacently, and he shrugged.

"Very well. Bring him. Let's see what he wants."

Fion entered in his best clothes. There was the fine, white blouse of Irish linen Elaine and I had repaired for him, new leggings of soft leather, and a dark-green mantle of good Welsh wool. He walked without a splint now, and the leg had knit straight, although it pained him to wear a boot on it for long.

He bowed low before King Pellinore, and then before the ladies, and last before the royal courier.

"Good King Pellinore, I have been a prisoner and hostage in your home for three months now, and I have been treated like an honored guest. Such hospitality is amazing to one such as I, bred in a less sophisticated land, especially as I know well I have done nothing to deserve it. I feel I must do something for you, my lord, besides allow my relations to send you gold." He paused, to judge how it was going. King Pellinore seemed pleased and the courier stunned. Queen Alyse waited expectantly.

"There is not much that is in my power to do, I admit. But I am young, I am unwed, and promised to no woman. I am my father's only heir. It would please me, and I hope do you honor, to make one of your household my wife and future Queen of Ireland."

King Pellinore's jaw dropped, and then he grinned broadly. "I call that a handsome offer, lad. Which one of them do you want?"

Fion bowed low. "Sir, with humble respect, I ask for the hand of your daughter, the beautiful Elaine."

Elaine gasped. Alyse looked scandalized. With an effort, I made my face an expressionless mask—it was best; everyone expected me to look hurt, while I could barely contain my laughter. King Pellinore had opened his mouth to accept him when Alyse cut in.

"Pellinore, this is not a thing to be taken lightly, nor discussed in public. It is up to Elaine to decide, and she should be given time. She is young to leave home. I—I would have thought, sir," she addressed herself coolly to Fion, "that there are those among the king's household of a riper age for marriage than my daughter. Honor would still be conferred."

"Perhaps so, gracious lady," Fion replied with a glint in his eye, "but none but Princess Elaine could I ask to be my wife." He left it at that, and there was nothing Alyse could say. But Pellinore was slower to catch on. He motioned Fion over to him and lowered his voice until he thought I could not hear him.

"If she's too young, what about my ward, Guinevere? She's as pretty as the other, if I do say it myself, and a mite older. Wouldn't she do as well, my lord?"

"With all due respect for yourself, sire, and with all respect and admiration for your ward, whose beauty has not passed unnoticed, I assure you, I can only offer for the Lady Elaine. I would be false to my heart to do otherwise."

"Well, well," Pellinore grumbled, pleased as punch at his reply, and tickled pink, I could see, at the thought of Elaine's being Queen of Ireland, "I'll not stand in your way. But it's up to my daughter, you know, and the queen seems not to favor it. Let me speak with them awhile."

"Thank you, my lord. There is—one more thing. I wonder if you would present me to King Arthur."

"If my daughter accepts you, you may be sure I shall. If not, on what grounds? You are my hostage, not his."

"So I am aware, my lord. But as I am to be King of Ireland, it is meet I should know the man with whom I shall have to deal. It matters not to me whether I come to him as hostage or free man, and I can't see that it would matter to him."

"Hmmm. I shall consider it. There is something in the suggestion. I leave day after tomorrow to join him; perhaps I shall discuss it with him then, if the Saxons give us leave."

Dinner ended swiftly after Fion left, and Alyse called us both into her chamber for a conference.

"Did you know about this, Guinevere?" she asked angrily.

"No, madam, indeed I did not."

"Why are you angry with Gwen, Mother? She has done nothing but been publicly spurned," Elaine protested, slipping an arm around my waist. "How can you blame her? She is to be pitied. Oh, Gwen, I'm so sorry I was jealous. All this time I thought he loved you, not me."

I shrugged. "There's no need for pity."

Alyse paced furiously across the chamber.

"I don't believe it for a minute," she snapped. "It's a clever plot, very clever. I've harbored a viper in my nest. The scoundrel! How dare he?"

Leonora and Cissa backed against the drapes. I kept my eyes on the floor.

"Mother!" Elaine cried. "Are you insulted at his proposal? You act so, and yet you want it for Gwen. I thought you would be proud."

Alyse shook her head. "Oh, Elaine, my dear. You cannot understand. It was an honorable enough proposal. I accuse him of being insincere. He offered for you because he knows you will reject him." A wave of fear swept her face. "You *will* reject him, Elaine."

"Yes, Mother."

"Had he offered for Gwen, he might have been accepted."

"I would not have accepted," I said quietly, to the floor.

"You are my ward. I might have accepted for you," Alyse replied, stiffening.

I looked up then. So she would not allow me my choice, after all. I think I had suspected it all along. I met her eyes squarely, and the relationship between us subtly changed and hardened into battle lines. "You could not have accepted for me."

Alyse bristled. "I am queen and your guardian. Tell my why I could not have accepted for you. It is the best you could ever do."

"Because," I said, the words dropping into the silence like stones into a still pool, "I am not yet a woman."

Alyse stared, then threw up her hands in resignation.

"Then perhaps it is just as well. You are old enough to be betrothed, and marriage could wait six months or longer. It cannot be that far off, at the rate you are growing. But as it stands, he has not offered, so I cannot accept."

"If you had accepted, I would not go."

The women gasped and held their breaths as Alyse flushed darkly. "You would go. Else you would be horsewhipped."

"I shall not leave Britain." I spoke with certainty, although it was only a blind faith in Fion's visions.

Alyse came up to me. I noticed that I was taller by a handspan and that there were gray hairs among the gold on her head. "Until you come into womanhood, niece, you will do exactly as I tell you. And when that blessed day arrives, I shall marry you off to the very first lord who looks at you twice. See if I don't. You are dismissed."

Back in our chamber, Elaine embraced me. "Gwen, I apologize for my mother. And I apologize for all my rude behavior. I have said things—you know which things—I did not mean. But I thought, all this time, that he loved you."

I lowered my eyes. "Thank you, Elaine. But he has not hurt my feelings, as everyone thinks. I knew he would not offer for me. So you see, I have lost nothing by it. And you have gained much. You have turned down the King of Ireland!"

She brightened and hugged me again. "Let's make a pact. We will swear by the Virgin never to fall in love with the same man. Is it agreed?"

The mischievous glint in her eye made me laugh. "Whoever sees him first, you mean? If I am ever to find a husband with you about, Elaine, I see I must practice my sprints!"

We laughed together, but I knew in my heart what she meant. I must take care from now on to keep well away from anyone Elaine admired. I was never again to be first in anyone's eyes. She would not forgive me twice.

Alyse and Pellinore did not sleep at all that night, by the look of them in the morning. And their arguments continued for the next two days. Pellinore was heard to exclaim that he didn't give a——if Elaine liked the lad or not. Queen of Ireland was good enough for him, and therefore good enough for her. If she persisted in refusing every suitor who came to her door, he would take matters into his own hands and contract her, sight unseen, to a lord of his choosing. Queen Alyse got round him somehow, though, for he was resigned to it by the time he left to meet Arthur.

Fion was left behind to nurse his disappointment. What he really thought we did not know, for we were forbidden to visit him any longer. But when we rode beneath his window, sometimes we heard him singing.

8 ❀ BETROThAL

A week after my fourteenth birthday, Merlin's prophecy was fulfilled, and I began to bleed. I shared my excitement only with Elaine, and together, with Ailsa's help, we kept it secret from Alyse. For although her anger had passed, she was not kind to me any longer, and all of us who had heard her threaten me believed her. King Pellinore, her only master, was still away at war; while he was gone her power was absolute.

Fion was kept to his room, and I missed his company. Even when I was out with Zephyr, which was where I loved best to be, I thought of him, now a true prisoner, with pity and regret. I even toyed with the idea of telling Alyse I would marry him if he asked me—he was a good companion, I knew he cared for me, and Ireland could not be so bad. Almost anything was better than this tension at home. But I knew, in my heart, he would not take me. By some strange logic he had convinced himself I was meant for something else. It made me want to laugh, had it not been so sad.

Then in the month of the summer solstice we had a messenger from King Pellinore. The fighting was done, and the Saxons turned back in a great victory. King Lot of Lothian had received his death blow there, and Merlin the Enchanter had been found living in a cave in the Caledonian Forest within a stone's throw of the battleground. King Pellinore would be home with his troops in a week's time, and we were to send messages to Ireland to bring gold for Fion's ransom and take him away.

The palace was thrown into sudden activity. Everything was made ready at once. The castle was cleaned from top to bottom, a great feast was prepared, hunts were organized for fresh game, wild flowering herbs were gathered and fashioned into wreaths, which we hung in every room to sweeten the air. In all the bustle I managed to visit Fion twice without being noticed.

The first time I went to thank him properly for his offer for Elaine. He kissed my cheek and replied it was the least he could do for the princess who saved his life. When I told him the great news, that the High King had been victorious and Merlin had been found alive, he replied that he had never doubted either event. The second time I went to see him was the day before Pellinore's return and his own departure. He was very solemn then, and excited, also. We said good-bye.

"I shall see you again, sweet Guinevere," he promised. "I shall come to your wedding."

I shuddered. "Don't talk about weddings, I pray you." And I told him what Queen Alyse had said.

He only smiled. "She can't do it. You will see. There are forces at work in this land that not even Queen Alyse can command. Open your eyes."

"What will you do when you are free?"

"To Ireland, I suppose, since the High King is away. And you?"

"What I always do in summer. Ride away from the castle as often as I can, on whatever excuse I can fashion."

"You should get yourself a falcon. That's all the excuse you need. Oh, Guinevere, this parting is more difficult than I expected."

He reached for me and pulled me up against him. He kissed my throat, and then my lips, and hugged me tightly. "Never forget you have a friend in Ireland. You need only send a word, and I will come to your aid."

His countrymen sailed in that evening and were reunited with him. King Pellinore arrived the next day with much fanfare. Everyone attended a great feast in the hall that night. The room was crowded with extra benches, and between the press of bodies and the flaring torches, it grew very warm.

The first piece of business was the ransoming of Fion. This was accomplished with great ceremony, and when it was done, and Fion was a free man, he was offered and accepted a seat of honor at the round table. Then King Pellinore gave an account of the battle against the Saxons and the finding of Merlin.

"He was wandering about fringes of the battlefield, his wits quite gone, giving directions to the soldiers. One of the captains bound him to a tree to keep him out of harm's way, but at battle's end when they went back to release him, he was gone, although the rope was there, with all the knots still tied. The soldiers were convinced he was an apparition, but the captain was not so sure.

He had been calling out the names of Ector, Kay, and Bedwyr, and Arthur's childhood name. When the High King heard this story, he left off his pursuit of Saxon stragglers and raced back to scour the forest."

The story Pellinore told of Arthur's reunion with his friend touched the heart of everyone in the hall. He found Merlin in a small, damp cave, dressed in skins, aged twenty years, gray-haired and feeble, and never left his side from the moment he arrived until the great magician opened his eyes and spoke his name, three days later. Then he wept and kissed him, and fed him broth with his own hands. Merlin recovered his wits, but had no recollection of what had happened to him last autumn, or of the time in between. Some said the rigors of the Caledonian winter had robbed him of his youth and vigor; some said it had to be the work of poison; others maintained this was just another shape that Merlin took, by his own choosing. So as things stood, no one knew why or how Merlin had disappeared, and Merlin himself said nothing.

There followed many toasts to King Arthur and some to Fion, and the hall began to get rowdy. Queen Alyse rose to lead the ladies out. But before we left, I heard Pellinore advise Fion that the High King was traveling south to Caerleon before going on to invest Caer Camel and would be passing along the eastern border of Wales in the next day or two. Fion's features lit with joy, and he thanked Pellinore for ransoming him, that he might meet the High King of Britain as a free man. He left the next day to catch the King along the Glevum road. What he thought of our young King we did not learn that season, for he returned along the northern route to Caer Narvon and took sail from there. But I heard later that within a day of their meeting, Prince Fion had sworn the future allegiance of Ireland to Arthur, and Arthur had sworn the present friendship and protection of Britain to the Gaels.

Caer Camel was invested that summer, and at last Britain had a center, a fighting fortress for her King and his fighting men. It lay in the middle of the Summer Country, the land of gently rolling downs and soft breezes where sheep graze year round, the air smells faintly of the salt marshes, and the signal fires on hill and tor give long warning of an enemy's approach. The Saxon hordes were quiet that summer. Rumor had it they were finally defeated or, on the other hand, that they were regrouping for one last desperate attack. Arthur of the Eleven Battles was ready for them. He spent that year reinforcing his defenses, reestablishing contact with all his vassal lords, settling territory disputes, and gathering to his side young men of fighting age who wished to join the King's Companions.

I followed Fion's suggestion and persuaded Pellinore to let me hawk. I think he pitied me, after my public rejection by Fion, and sensing the queen's mistrust of me afterward, determined to do me a kindness. He was a soft-hearted man, though his speech was blunt and his manner gruff. His falconer found me a young bird, which I trained as Gwarthgydd had taught me. I fashioned its jesses myself out of soft worked leather and then, to my consternation, discovered that Zephyr was terrified of the thing. It took two whole months to get her to accept the bird and to get her accustomed to being ridden without reins and following leg signals only. But eventually we three worked as a team, and my young falcon Ebon provided many a fat dove for the queen's supper, whether she knew it or not.

The next time I saw Fion was in the autumn of my fourteenth year. Gilomar had died that summer, and Fion was now King. He was on his way to Caer Camel to a meeting of all of Arthur's nobles and his allies, called by the Companions for the purpose of finding Arthur a wife. Pellinore himself was going and stayed his departure to wait for Fion and travel down with him to the Summer Country. The news of this great meeting spread like wildfire throughout the kingdoms, and every king who attended carried instructions from his lady to propose his daughter, or his granddaughter, or his niece or whomever among his kin was the most eligible. Bards were hired to sing poems extolling the beauties of this maid and that. Family lineages were hunted up and extended back to Roman governors, or Maximus if it was possible. Bargains were made among families for backing; friendships of long standing were broken in the heat of competition.

The only two people in the Kingdom who stood aloof from this frenzy were, oddly, the High King and myself. By all reports Arthur had no desire to remarry, but was aware of the necessity to produce an heir, and thus yielded to the pressure brought by his Companions. He was content to let his subjects make the choice for him. All he required in a bride, he had said, was an honest tongue and a soft voice. As for myself, even if I had had Elaine's ambition, which I did not, there was no one to speak for me. My parents were dead. My brothers had daughters of their own. My guardians were the parents of one of the most eligible maidens in the land, and one who desired nothing more than the very position that needed filling. At last, it seemed, the world was marching to

Elaine's tune. This, she told me in secret, as if it were news, was what she had been born for. She was sure of it.

Indeed, in the new gown she wore to Fion's welcome feast, she looked every inch a queen. With her dark gold hair bound with flowers, her dancing, sky-blue eyes, her milky skin, and willowy figure, she could have passed for a woman of twenty, although she was but thirteen. Even Fion stared. He was still unmarried, but it was too late to renew his suit for Elaine. The only topic at dinner that night was the searching of Britain for Arthur's bride, and Elaine positively glowed. When Pellinore announced his intention to propose Elaine to the High King, the hall stood up and cheered. Elaine squeezed my hand hard under the table, and although she cast down her eyes as a maid should, her look was triumphant. I kissed her cheek affectionately and caught Fion looking at us thoughtfully.

When the noise in the hall had abated somewhat, I turned to Fion. "My lord Fion, the last time we saw you, you were on your way to make your peace with our King. Pray tell us how you found him: Were you treated honorably? Did you get fair hearing?"

"I have never met a more honorable man, fair lady," Fion replied solemnly. "Your King was graciousness itself. He heard me out until I had nothing more to say. He knew who I was, but he did not hold my father's sins against me. By the questions he asked, I saw he had a thorough knowledge of our shore defenses and knew something of the rivalries among our petty kings. I do not know how he gets his information, or how he has the time to think of Ireland with the Saxons at his back, but he understood how the land lay all about him, and he welcomed me most honorably. He made me feel like a brother." He paused. Pellinore was nodding with a broad smile on his face, and Elaine's eyes were shining. "He speaks to the lowliest of his servants with consideration. Every man has respect at Arthur's table. Were my heart not in Ireland, I would lay it at his feet."

Every man in the hall rose cheering, and there were many shouts of "Arthur!" and "Fion!" I was moved by his testimonial. Elaine was beside herself with excitement.

"You see, Gwen," she whispered to me, "he really is what he is supposed to be! I have known it my entire life!"

So she had. Elaine had never lost her faith in Arthur. She had believed every wondrous tale she had heard about him, and Fion's words were only fuel to her fire. I prayed hard that night that God would grant her her wish, even if it meant Alyse took us all to live at court.

Everyone knows what happened, of course. It is difficult to look back over the span of years and remember the uproar of those days. The meeting, which had been planned to last a week in order that everyone could speak, stretched to two weeks, and then three. There were too many candidates, and a consensus could not be found. Every leading family in the land had a daughter or a niece of marriageable age. Every maid had a flawless lineage, flawless complexion, flawless eyes of black, brown, blue, green, gray; flawless hair of gold, brown, black, red; features of surpassing beauty, an honest tongue and a lovely voice. Even Arthur wearied of it and went hawking. Feuds developed, powerful leaders backed one family and then another as the offers of gold increased. Happy was the man who had nothing to gain or lose by the King's decision. And throughout it all, Merlin sat by the High King's chair, old and frail, his black eyes watching it all, saying nothing.

At last, his patience near an end, King Arthur commanded the meeting to close. He would not divide his Kingdom over a woman, he said. He would rather die unwed. Only then did a young man rise from the rear of the Welsh delegation and, having received permission to speak, addressed the High King in a trembling voice. Just as silver was found threaded into black rock deep within the earth, he began, just as gold was sprinkled sparsely over pebbled sands, so all treasures worth pursuing did not come easy; the brightest jewel often lay buried in the darkest clay. As he overcame his fear, his voice fell into the sweet singsong of the storyteller, and the Welshmen in the hall settled back comfortably to hear his tale. It was, it seems, the tale of the emperor Maximus and how he found his Elen, the famous Welsh beauty with sapphire eyes whom Maximus wed and for whom he forswore allegiance to Rome. She was, he sang, fairer than the stars among the heavens, more constant than the sun in his course across the sky, sweeter than wildflowers that grace the summer meadows, and ever a true companion to the king. In all his endeavors she was beside him; she brought him luck and victory; he never lost a battle until he left Britain, where she could not follow. The singer paused—Welshmen were wont to attribute Maximus' prowess to the virtues of his Welsh wife, but it was unwise to expect this descendant of Maximus to believe it—he claimed, instead, that hidden in the dark Welsh mountains lay a jewel as bright as Elen, a girl as beautiful, as wise and steadfast, as Maximus' own bride. Like a vein of precious metal lying undiscovered in the hills, she awaited the High King's notice; a word from him could bring her gold to light. A king's daughter she was, descended from Elen, with hair of starlight and the voice of a nightingale. And Gwillim, for it was my old childhood companion who had risen to speak before them all, took a deep breath and held hard to his courage. The maiden's name, he said, was Guinevere.

There was a shocked silence. The Companions froze. Arthur's face was a mask. Merlin closed his eyes. Then the throng found their voices, and angry protests arose on all sides. "How dare the boy?" "What maid is this? I have heard no tell of her." "That he should mention the name before the king!" Then Gwarthgydd rose and clapped a hand on Gwillim's shoulder.

"My lords," he said, and his deep rumbling voice got their attention. "The lad speaks of my half-sister, Guinevere of Northgallis. In his later years, my father the King of Northgallis wed Elen of Gwynedd, a beauty of renown. She died giving birth to the lady in question, who was a childhood friend of Gwillim's here. She is now the ward of King Pellinore and Queen Alyse and lives in Gwynedd. Gwillim likes a good tale, but all he has said is true enough."

"Is that the Lark of Gwynedd?" someone asked. "I have heard of her."

"Isn't that the maid the old witch prophesied about, the night of her birth? You remember Giselda—"

"A curse, I thought it was, a spell—"

"Oh, no, she prophesied great beauty and great fame—"

"Has anyone seen her?" one of the Companions asked. "Where is Pellinore? Who can attest to the lad's claims?"

But Pellinore, weary of words, was out hunting. It was Fion who stood.

That winter lasted forever. Elaine lay abed with an illness born of disappointment and envy, and Alyse could barely tolerate the sight of me. Pellinore was proud and conscious of his new status in the High King's inner circle, but he never came to the women's quarters, wishing to avoid Alyse's cold fury at his betrayal, and I saw him only at dinner in the evenings. The queen's ladies kept aloof at the queen's wishes. Only Ailsa, of all the women in the castle, was thoroughly excited on my behalf.

"Just think of it! Wouldn't your dear mother be proud! Her little Gwen to be King Arthur's Queen! Why, I just pinch myself when I think of it! How lucky you are, my lady! How happy you will be!"

But I could not see how this unexpected event could make me happy. Already it seemed to have cost me Elaine's friendship, and she was the only real friend I had ever had. Proud as I was to be chosen out of all the maids in Britain, I could not envision happiness ahead. I was to be married to a man I had never met, and because he was who he was, there was no possible way out of it. I did not feel the thrill all Britain expected me to feel; I felt only apprehension and a nagging regret that I had not married Fion.

However much she suffered at the sight of me, Alyse knew her duty. She set all her ladies to work on my wardrobe, and we sat together all winter sewing my wedding clothes, fashioning new gowns, weaving bed linens and chamber hangings. Dear Pellinore ended up spending Fion's ransom on my trousseau. For if I did not go to Arthur surrounded by the most luxurious finery in the kingdom, I would shame Wales. We had the long winter to get ready, for in the spring the King would come himself to take me out of Wales.

I put this from my mind, for I shook with fear at the very thought of it. Wales was the only home I knew. I remembered every word I had ever spoken to Elaine about how dreadful it would be to be Arthur's Queen—well, I thought, I was justly served. That horrible witch had been proved right. And poor Gwillim, who I am sure thought he was doing me the finest service of his life, had been the unwitting instrument of my undoing. But there was nothing to do but face it. If I opened my mouth in complaint, I would shame Alyse and Pellinore, I would shame Northgallis, I would shame Wales. So I said very little and let the people take my silence for maidenly modesty if they chose.

In the month before the equinox Elaine finally rose from her bed. She was thin and pale and took the chair closest to the fire, but at least she joined us.

"Gwen," she said on our first night together in four months, "please forgive me for my grief. I wish you all happiness, you know that. I hated you for a while, but that was my unruly jealousy. I have remembered the prophecy at your birth, and also Merlin's prophecy, and I know that it is you who were born for this, and not I. Please forgive me."

"Oh, Elaine!" I threw my arms around her and we cried together for a long time. "Dear cousin, I would give anything in the world to change places with you and give you your heart's desire!

stallion was interested in the mare, but he controlled the animal effortlessly, without thought, with legs and seat and hand, as fluidly and as softly as the horse himself moved. It must give pleasure to the horse, I thought, to be ridden with such skill.

As we approached the castle, the woods gave way to fields, and I glanced mischievously at Lancelot. "Would my lord care to follow me? I know a shorter way back, but there are obstacles."

He hesitated, aware of the challenge. "Obstacles for a horse, my lady, or obstacles for a man?"

I laughed. "Follow me, my lord, and find out."

He glanced swiftly behind him and nodded. "Lead on."

I took them to my jumping field where I had, over time, fashioned a formidable series of obstacles. I settled Ebon on my arm and sang softly to him for reassurance, for this was new to him. Then I put Zephyr into a light gallop, and we flew over the obstacles. I gloried in the sensation of hurtling through the air, with the salt sea breeze in my face and my hair whipping behind me. I felt like a prisoner granted a last day of freedom before execution, and this was it—my last taste of girlhood. At the top of the field, I cantered the mare in a circle and then brought her to a halt. All three knights were standing where I had left them, watching me. I waited. It had been easy for us, we had done it before. But although the fences were new to them, the animals they rode were trained warhorses, stronger than Zephyr and as nimble, who knew maneuvers on a field of battle and could be a third weapon under a good rider. Lancelot was a horseman. We should see about the others.

Lancelot gathered his stallion and cantered toward the first fence. The stallion shied, but then obeyed and pushed himself over. At the next brush pile he took off too far out and barely missed landing upon it. By the third fence Lancelot had learned to judge the distance, and every obstacle thereafter was an improvement upon the one before. At length he drew up beside me, breathing hard, eyes shining.

"By heaven, that is a sport for kings! My compliments to Pellinore for building it, and to your own skill, my lady—the bird never stirred from your arm!"

"Pellinore had nothing to do with it," I retorted. "It was my own idea. I like to jump. And as for Ebon, he trusts me."

He stared. "My compliments to you, then, Lady Guinevere. But surely he built it for you."

"Certainly not. He disapproves of my jumping. I built it myself."

"By God!" he cried, his eyes dancing, "You are one woman in a thousand!"

I looked away to avoid looking into his eyes. "Am I odd, then? I do not wish to be."

"You are perfect! Perfectly suited to the High King, I mean." I was watching the others when he spoke, and heard in his voice the tenderness I had seen already in his face. I wished with all my heart that he would stop reminding me of Arthur. I did not know then that he was reminding himself.

Bedwyr made a good attempt. His horse refused the obstacle at first, but he persevered and got him over. All was then well until he came to the hen coop, where the stallion slid to a stop at the last moment and tossed Bedwyr over. Kay, who refused the challenge altogether, cantered over to him.

"What manner of man is Kay of Galava?"

Lancelot smiled. "He's old for his age and always has been. He's Arthur's seneschal. His place is at Caer Camel, and he misses it. He worries about it every minute he's away. Since he was injured at Caer Eden his sword arm is weak, and as he cannot take the field for Arthur, he holds his fortress in readiness. It is his service, and he is devoted."

It was clear from his tone of voice that Kay was valued for his devotion.

"He frowns upon my hawking."

Lancelot shrugged. "He believes that women should ride litters, not horses, and should be rocking cradles, not hunting falcons. It is his way."

I plucked nervously at Zephyr's mane. "And the High King?"

"What about the High King?"

"Does he disapprove of women hawking?"

Lancelot turned toward me, amused. "Do I hear aright? Are you actually frightened of Arthur?"

I raised my chin in defiance. "Do you blame me, my lord? I have heard so much and know so little."

He laughed outright, and I bit my lip, blushing. "My dear Guinevere, Pendragon may be feared by Saxons, and rightly so, but *you* have no need to be afraid. Do you imagine him a cruel tyrant? He is the kindest man in all the kingdoms. Why, Arthur would no sooner keep you from hawking or doing whatever it was you pleased than he would cut off his nose to spite his face. He would laugh at the very idea!"

He filled me with relief. "Then I shall be allowed to keep Zephyr? Is this truth, Lancelot? It has worried me a long time."

He began to look astonished. "Of course you may keep her. He is not a monster, Guinevere. Your doubts disturb me. Is not the High King known among his people here in Wales?"

"How a King treats his people is one thing. How a man treats his—his wife may be quite another."

He grew instantly grave and nodded. "That is true. I forgot myself, my lady. But with Arthur it is the same thing. The man and the King are one."

I looked into his face and saw his own devotion there. Clearly Arthur was a great leader, to inspire love in such different men as Kay and Lancelot.

Bedwyr rode up then, with Kay behind him, and I apologized sincerely for putting them through my little game. It had been a long winter, I told them, with nothing for maids to do but sew and listen to women's gossip. The high spirits of spring had to be played out in some fashion. They forgave me like the gentlemen they were; no one reminded me of my promise to be ladylike; and we approached the castle yard as princess and royal escort, much to Kay's relief.

Elaine was aghast. "Oh, Gwen, how could you! All these months we have been preparing for this visit, and their first sight of you is bareback upon your horse, in those filthy leggings! And your hair is flying everywhere! Oh, what must they think?"

I grinned at her as Ailsa pulled the shift down over my head. "My leggings are not filthy. I brush them well after every ride."

"Oh, don't, Gwen. Think of the report will they send to King Arthur!"

Ailsa sat me on the stool and began to brush my hair. I took Elaine's hand.

"Forgive me. I see this affects you deeply. But truly," I said, smiling as I thought of Lancelot standing rooted in the clearing, "I am not worried about the report they will send to King Arthur."

She looked puzzled. "I see you are not. But for goodness' sake, why not?"

"Never mind. I am bathed and clean now, dear Elaine, and Ailsa will dress my hair, and I shall wear the blue gown you embroidered with wildflowers, and I promise I will be a lady and try to make a good impression."

"I should hope so," she said crossly. "It's important to Mother. And to me. You must be—that is, you must try to be—"

"Perfect," I finished for her, sadly. "As everyone says Arthur is."

She nodded. "I guess so. I suppose it's a lot to ask."

I fought off panic as the weight of responsibility descended upon me once again. "It's far too much to ask. And everyone in Britain expects it. But at least I shall not be alone." I was thinking of Lancelot, who had become my friend so quickly.

Elaine kissed my cheek. "I shall be there as long as you are, Gwen. Rely on it."

Startled, I thanked her, and covered my confusion with some question about the progress of the trousseau. She answered with eagerness and filled me in on all the things I had missed while I was out—principally the arrival of the King's men. I listened, but my thoughts drifted back to the clearing, and to the jumping field, and to a pair of clear gray eyes and serious black brows.

"Dress my hair with the little pearls and bluebells, Ailsa," I said suddenly. "I wish to look my best tonight."

Ailsa looked at me sharply, and Elaine smiled.

"Now I know what's different about you today," she said. "You are finally happy. You have been happy ever since you came in."

"Have I?" I avoided Ailsa's eyes. "Well, perhaps so. It was a glorious day."

Queen Alyse led us into the greeting hall, where Pellinore waited with the King's Companions. The mellow evening light filtered in through the open windows and picked out the jewels the men wore on shoulder, belt, and wrist. They were weaponless, for Pellinore followed the High King's practice of leaving all weapons outside the meeting hall, except for the short dagger needed to cut food. King Pellinore presented Queen Alyse and Elaine; the courtiers bowed low. Lancelot wore a dark blue tunic of plain, fine wool. The silver buckle on his belt was worked in the shape of a hawk with wings outspread. He stood half a head taller than Pellinore, who was not considered a small man. Even as I looked at him, he dipped one knee to the floor and kissed my hand.

"King Arthur's compliments, my lady," he said formally. "He has sent us poor soldiers in his stead, not because he did not want to come, but because he could not."

"So I understand, my lord."

"He has sent me with words of greeting and begs for your forgiveness of his most untimely absence."

"He is High King. My lord, I understand."

"He would rather be here in Wales with you, my lady, than riding north to look at Saxons. He told me this himself."

"Where Britain needs him most, there must the High King go," I replied. "My lord may tell him he is forgiven." At last, it seemed, I had said the right thing. Kay and Bedwyr were nodding, pleased.

"And he bade me present you with this gift," Lancelot continued, "in the hope that it might ease your anger toward him and incline you to look favorably upon him."

Lancelot proffered a small packet, wrapped in soft linen. But I forbore to take it from him.

"Good Sir Lancelot. You speak as if Pendragon were one suitor among many. I do assure you, my lord, that I look with favor upon the High King so long as he holds the Saxons at bay. There is no cause for anger. He need send no gifts to win me. I know wherein my duty lies."

Kay and Bedwyr were positively beaming. Alyse looked at me in wonder, hardly able to credit me capable of a diplomatic word.

When he spoke, Lancelot's voice was low and gentle. "Will my lady not accept it, then, as a token of the King's esteem?"

I smiled at him. "I would be honored to accept a token of the King's esteem, my lord."

Lancelot opened the soft wrappings and lifted from them a single sapphire set in silver, the size of a robin's egg, and hung from a silver chain. It glowed in the evening light, dark blue and deep and clear. Lancelot came up to me and put his arms around my shoulders as he fastened it behind my neck. By sheer effort of will I stilled my trembling and stared hard past his shoulder at Kay, but I felt his breath on my skin, and then the warm touch of his hands as he struggled with the clasp. I felt it then for the first time—the hot lick of fire that set me ablaze with an emotion I did not then understand. He hesitated and leaned closer. "It is the color of your eyes," he whispered in my ear, and stepped back slowly. I sank to the floor in a low curtsy, shaking, which sent light glittering off the great sapphire.

"Please—please tell King Arthur I am overwhelmed," I managed.

Elaine and Alyse crowded round to view the stone and chatter in admiration. I was glad for their protection while I recovered my composure. I could not meet his eyes; it was like looking into flame. At last Pellinore offered me his arm and took me into dinner. Lancelot followed with Queen Alyse, and Kay with Elaine. At dinner, Pellinore placed me beside Lancelot, his foremost guest of honor.

As the wine was passed around, Bedwyr gave what news there was of the state of the Kingdom, but for once I was not attentive. I looked everywhere about me, at the troopers, Pellinore's and the

High King's, eating together in the hall, at the bowl of jonquils and bluebells at the center of the round table, at the bodice of Elaine's yellow gown, which I had embroidered with stars. Look where I might, I was conscious only of the man beside me, of the grip of his long fingers around the winecup, the turning of his head toward the speaker, the stillness of his body in his chair.

King Pellinore was proposing a series of hunts for the Companions to keep them busy while we finished the trousseau. To this Kay and Bedwyr readily agreed.

Then Lancelot spoke. "I have one favor to ask of you, Pellinore. Give me two hours each day to spend with the young princesses. The High King appreciates that leaving home to marry a man one has never seen may be hard on a young maid and he does not wish to meet Lady Guinevere as a stranger. He has instructed me to tell her aught she wishes to know about him and the life we lead at Caer Camel. If the young ladies are willing, I beg your permission to fulfill the High King's desire."

Kay and Bedwyr looked surprised, and it made me wonder if Lancelot had made the whole thing up. But Elaine looked ecstatic, and Pellinore of course agreed, so it was settled.

As dinner progressed and conversation became general, I gathered my courage and turned to Lancelot. "Forgive my impertinence, my lord, but did you speak the truth about the High King just now?"

He smiled. "Does my lady suspect me of inventing ways to spend more time in her presence?"

I flushed scarlet, I could feel the heat in my face, but his look was tender.

"It was truth, my lady. He spoke so only to me, but it is truly his desire to ease what fears you have of him. And I know now that you have them." He lowered his gaze to his plate, and his voice went low. "But had he not said so, I would have invented it. Your suspicions are just."

I felt triumphant and weak all at once and struggled to keep my voice steady. "I am glad you included Elaine. She is a great admirer of Arthur's."

He raised his eyes to me then and looked at me long and directly. "And so will you be, Guinevere, in time."

I bowed my head.

Lancelot kept his word. Whatever the men were doing, hunting, hawking, drilling troops, he took time out every day to spend with Elaine and me. In the beginning all the queen's ladies crowded round him to hear him speak of Arthur, but eventually, as the day of departure grew near and the trousseau lay unfinished, they kept to the sewing room, and we had just Leonora for chaperone. Elaine was almost always with me. On the four or five occasions when Lancelot and I went riding, we took several of Pellinore's men along for escort and said very little to one another. And every time we spoke, Lancelot was careful to bring King Arthur between us, gently and firmly. In my mind's eye I saw him as our guardian, and in this I was not far off the mark.

When we sat together, usually in the queen's garden, it was always Elaine who asked about Arthur.

"What is the truth of his birth?" Elaine wanted to know. "Why did no one ever see him? Where did Merlin hide him?"

Lancelot smiled. "In spite of the rumors that I know run rampant, Merlin did not spirit him away to a far-off land, nor change him into an eagle. He grew up in Galava, with Sir Ector as his foster father and Kay his brother. No one noticed him because he was not specially treated. When he traveled with Ector, he went not as a prince of the land but as a minor noble's son in Ector's protection, with small escort and smaller fanfare. Ector, a brave soldier who fought with Ambrosius, and a kind man, took him into his household for fostering when he was just a baby. Arthur and Kay grew up as brothers." The source of Kay's devotion lay revealed, and also of his readiness to disapprove of me.

"But where was Merlin all this time?" Elaine wondered. "I thought he raised the King himself."

Lancelot smiled at her, but Elaine seemed unaffected. "So people say, but Merlin himself has never said so. And yet there is some truth in the claim. Behind the scenes, Merlin supervised the prince's education and kept track of him through the power of his Sight. He sometimes lived as a holy hermit in the forest above Count Ector's castle. There he would meet the boy and give him lessons and tell him the story of his begetting and his lineage, as if it all pertained to someone else. You might remember," Lancelot continued, "Uther Pendragon proclaimed throughout Britain that he would not acknowledge the son he begot at Tintagel. Thus neither Ector nor Merlin could in all fairness tell him who he was."

"But how was his true birth kept from him?" I asked. "I have always found that part of the tale difficult to believe. Sir Ector must have told him something."

"But it is true, my lady. He did not know. Ector told him his parents were of noble birth, but that they could not claim him. Arthur assumed he was the bastard of some petty lord, and Kay his superior in birth and breeding. He heard all the tales about Prince Arthur that you have heard, but he never once thought they might apply to him."

"But the name!" Elaine exclaimed. "And to have Merlin the Enchanter as a teacher! I'd have guessed, if it had been me!"

"Ah, but 'Arthur' was not his name." Lancelot turned to me and smiled. My breath caught in my throat. "Sometime when he is deep in thought and not attending, call 'Emreis' softly, and judge the truth yourself by the unthinking quickness of his response." I colored and looked down. "As for Merlin," Lancelot continued gently, "he is a master at disguise. He transformed himself so completely into a wild holy man that Ector himself barely knew him. As Arthur had never seen him, it really is no wonder he did not guess."

"Well, why is Merlin so dear to him, then," Elaine objected, with a shake of her bountiful curls, "if Sir Ector was his foster father?"

"Perhaps because he valued more the things that Merlin taught him." Lancelot shrugged. "Or perhaps it is just the chance agreement of two personalities." He shot me a swift glance and looked away. I blushed uncontrollably.

"It may have been so for his childhood," Elaine went on, "but surely, by the time he went to Caer Eden to fight for the High King, he must have guessed. Holy men are not so wise as Merlin and never stay so long in one place."

Suddenly I saw what lay ahead and attempted to steer the conversation another way, but Elaine would not have it. She pressed Lancelot to answer.

"Ah, but Arthur did not know that. Galava is a small place, and his experience of wandering holy men was limited to one."

"Then surely he must have guessed when Ector armed him for the battle. He was by rights too young to be a warrior."

Lancelot smiled, unaware of the bog ahead. "While it is true that Ector brought him on Uther's orders, it does not surprise me that Arthur did not guess. Think of the long years he had believed himself to be only a fosterling. And Galava is not far from Caer Eden. Had the Saxons won, his 'homeland' would have been directly threatened. He would have thought it strange had Ector *not* taken every able-bodied man and boy at his command, especially as Arthur, even at thirteen, was the best swordsman in Galava."

Elaine sighed in resignation. "Then it's true, after all, that Uther waited until the last minute to declare him?"

Still Lancelot went on, unseeing. "I have heard it was Uther's intention to talk to the boy and reveal his identity to him before the battle, but the Saxons attacked unexpectedly, and there was no time."

I looked down at my hands, twisted together in my lap. "And when, my lord, did he learn the truth?"

There was a long silence, and at last I glanced up. Lancelot looked stricken, having seen the pitfall too late. Elaine, in her innocence, merely waited for his answer. He cleared his throat and spoke stiffly.

"Uther told him the next day he was his father, in a public declaration, as he lay dying." When it was too late, I thought bitterly, *after* he had lain with his half-sister. Lancelot's eyes met mine, and he saw that I knew the tale, and I saw that the tale was true. If I felt grief, it was nothing to what Lancelot felt, having brought it upon me. Elaine continued unawares.

"You speak as if you were there, my lord. Did you attend, or did you hear these things from King Arthur?"

"I—I was there, my lady. I was young for it, just fourteen. I accompanied my father. He was convinced that our future lay with Britain, and he brought me over to fight at his side for Uther. He was wounded in the battle and, when he recovered, went home. I stayed to serve the new King." He spoke absently, his attention focused on what he had not said.

The conversation lagged, for we had heard about the battle, and at length Elaine excused herself. Leonora sat nodding in the sun. I leaned toward Lancelot.

"These are heavy matters, Lancelot," I whispered. "What has the High King said to you about it?"

Lancelot took a deep breath. "He has never spoken about it to anyone at all. Unless to Merlin. It is a subject the whole court avoids. I—I did not know you knew."

"I have heard rumors only. I have told no one."

He met my eyes. "Can you forgive him this, Guinevere? It is a great sin. It would be within your right to refuse him for this. No one could hold it against you."

"But—then the whole Kingdom would know for certain," I said softly.

He nodded and touched my hand. "Yes. But Arthur would survive it."

I rose unsteadily and went to the parapet. Lancelot followed. "Before I answer, there is another question I must ask you. Since you love him, I know what you will say. But you must, you *mus* tell me the truth."

Lancelot took both my hands in his. "I will not lie to you," he whispered. "I swear it by most holy God."

My whole body shook with fear at the risk I took, but somehow I found the courage to ask him. "Did Arthur kill the children a Dunpelder?"

Lancelot went white and stepped back, but his grip upon my hands was firm. "No. Never."

"Everyone thinks he did."

"No one who knows him thinks so."

"That is not an answer. Perhaps you do not know him well enough."

Anger darkened his eyes. "I know him better than I know myself. It is not in him. He did not do it."

"Has he said so? To you?"

"Yes."

"Who did the deed, then?"

"He does not know. But it must have been either Lot or Morgause herself." He spoke the woman's name reluctantly, as if it left a bad taste in his mouth.

"Then why do the rumors persist, if he is innocent?"

Lancelot shrugged. His face was cold. "Blame must land somewhere. The Witch of Orkney has seen to it that it fell on him."

I struggled to hold back the final accusation, but it was a moment of truth between us, and it came out. "He stood to gain so much."

Lancelot's features twisted in revulsion; still, he held my hands. "No one ever gains by killing children. The crime itself leaves a stain upon the soul. Had Arthur done it, he would not be the man he is now."

I exhaled in relief, and warmth returned to his face. "But this other evil—you admit his guilt. Has that deed not left a mark upon his soul?"

Lancelot's hands tightened around my own. "Indeed it has. So deep a mark, he will never be healed of it. That is why he cannot bear to hear her mentioned, though she is his kin. If you dare, you can make him talk about the massacre at Dunpelder. But you will never hear him speak the name 'Morgause.' " Lancelot paused and dropped my hands. "You must decide, Gwen, if you can forgive him. You must decide now. If you wish to withdraw, I must get the word out soon."

I looked down, hopelessly torn. Lancelot had offered me a way out, had opened the door, and now stood aside like a gentleman to let me go through, if I would. But what was beyond that door, I could not see. A tarnished Arthur, for certain. What would the people of Britain do when they knew the truth as I now knew it? What would Lancelot think of me if I refused? I felt a sob rise in my throat and squeezed my eyes shut. I knew what I must do.

I gathered my courage and met his eyes again, clear and gray and trusting. "It was done in ignorance," I whispered. "One should not be punished for ignorance. I know I feel it is unjust when it is done to me. So I should not be honest with myself if I held it against the High King."

Lancelot flung himself to his knees and clutched my hand, pressing it to his lips. "O noble heart!" he cried. "What forbearance is this in one so young and unworldly? May God in His Heaven bless you, I believe you are worthy of him!"

"What's this? What's this?" Leonora cried, waking suddenly. "What's happened here?"

Lancelot jumped to his feet, coloring, and bowed in her direction. "If I am out of turn, good Leonora, please forgive me. Lady Guinevere has just revealed her noble soul, and I have thanked her on the King's behalf."

Then he turned and fled. Leonora looked at me in bewilderment.

"Don't ask," I said wearily. "It's too much to tell. Come, let's get in out of this hot sun."

10 ❀ the parting

The day of departure approached. I noted that Ailsa said very little to me and clutched her amulets a great deal. Even Elaine, whom I expected to show increasing excitement, watched me worriedly. I had no idea what about me concerned them.

On the last day of May I finished the bridegroom's gift. I had thought long and hard over what I could give a King who had gifts beyond counting, and finally decided that it must be something I made myself. I took some fine white wool, lined it with white silk, and fashioned it into a day robe, such as King Pellinore wore when illness or bad weather kept him indoors. But I wanted to make it finer and more comfortable, for surely warriors must enjoy a change from leather and mail. This was a plain shift, warm enough for all but the coldest days, with soft silk next to the skin. It could be worn loose or belted and was edged in dark blue so as not to show dirt. Over the left breast I embroidered a design of my own invention: interlocking squares in the Celtic pattern, stitched in blue, forming a square turned on end; and within, the Red Dragon of Britain standing on hind feet, clawing the air. And above it all, in the tiniest of stitches for which my work was best known, a silver star to represent the kingstar that had lighted in the west the night of Arthur's begetting. And that was all. The rest of the garment was without ornament, simple and fine. Elaine was after me for weeks to add some decoration to the sleeves, or along the hemline, but I refused. It would not be my gift, if it was not as I liked it.

I showed it to no one but Elaine and Ailsa. We packed it carefully in cloth wrappings, and then within a box, and it was placed with my traveling chests that were already in readiness. Then King Pellinore, who had been chuckling secretly for weeks, revealed his wedding gift to the High King. His carpenters had fashioned for Arthur another round table, three times as large as the one in Pellinore's hall. It broke down into sections for ease of transport and to enable it to be taken through doorways, but he displayed it proudly to us all before it was disassembled. It was made of white oak and sanded and polished until it shone like glass. It could easily seat thirty men and could do double duty as a dinner table, or in the council chamber. The Companions were impressed and complimented Pellinore until his poor head was swollen with pride. Alyse declared it would take months to get him back in line.

As the day of departure neared, I should have been nervous, but I felt instead both exhilarated and terrified. One evening Elaine and I took Lancelot up to the western tower to watch the sun set over the sea. The sky was aflame with light, and we watched in silence as the red streaks burned purple and the evening star blazed forth.

"I shall miss Wales," I said softly. Elaine turned to me, and I saw there were tears in her eyes.

"I've always lived in sight of the sea," she exclaimed. "I cannot imagine what life will be like without it."

"Caer Camel is not far from the sea," Lancelot offered. "You cannot see it from the towers, but you can see the signal fires on the tor of Ynys Witrin, which sits on the Lake of Avalon, which is fed by the sea tides."

It was not the same, but no one said so. Lancelot seemed subdued.

"Has there been any news from the north?" I asked.

"There has been no fighting, my lady. The High King and his allies have shown the Saxons a strong front. I believe they are working on a treaty and on strengthening the line of defenses."

"There is no new word on when—when—" I could not finish, so Lancelot finished for me.

"No. My instructions are to take you to Caer Camel and there await him."

I nodded. In the darkness, Lancelot took my hand. Elaine had her handkerchief to her face, and Leonora had not wished to make the climb. I breathed out slowly as excitement and longing filled me. I now understood what I had only felt on the first day of his visit. In a month's time he had become more precious to me than life. His touch inflamed me, his smile robbed me of breath. Each night I dreamed I stood in his embrace, and each morning I awoke yearning for his kiss. And I knew that he felt the same. It was exhilarating, agonizing, thrilling, almost overwhelming, but it also hurt more than daggers, and all at the same time. So we stood in silence, hand in hand, in the beauty of the long June evening, loving without hope, and thinking of Arthur.

In bed that night, Elaine put her arms around me and said, "I know now, Gwen. I know why you've been so happy and so sad, and why you are not nervous about leaving, and why you so dread Arthur. You love Lancelot."

"Please, Elaine—"

"I shall never tell a soul. I was angry with you, though, until I saw that you could not help it, any more than I could. But what are we to do, Gwen?"

I gripped her by the wrists. "There is nothing to be done."

"Is there no way to talk to them and come to some agreement? That you may take Lancelot, and I Arthur?"

"No!" I cried, the tears that had been kept back at such cost all day finally bursting forth. "No, there is not! Think, Elaine! Arthur is High King of Britain, and Lancelot his second-in-command. The honor of all Britain is in our hands! Use your head! We are merely women."

"But—but it seems so unfair!"

"Yes. It is unfair. To you, to me, to Lancelot; most of all, to the King himself. But I truly don't see what is to be done about it. We must bear it. That is all."

"And if I can't bear it?" Elaine cried in despair.

"Elaine, you must!" I had a sudden prevision that filled me with horror. "Elaine, attend me! You must make me a promise— when we get to Caer Camel, you must behave as if you care nothing about the King. You must pretend that you dislike him. Be polite but always, always cool. Don't follow him with your eyes, don't put yourself in his way—you know what I mean. Everyone's honor depends on it. Will you promise?"

Elaine wept. "What you ask is impossible and you know it!"

"It is no more than I must do toward Lancelot. I know it is hard, but we are strong. You *have* to do it. It is the only way."

"You ask too much. I cannot promise."

"Then," I said slowly, "you cannot come."

She gasped. "You cannot prevent me! Mother has given me permission!"

"I can send you home with her when the celebrations are over. I will be Queen then. Even your mother must be obedient to my command."

Elaine went suddenly still and silent. Her tears dried but her body trembled. For a long time she said nothing. I waited in wretchedness, remembering Gwillim kneeling at my bed, sacrificing his friendship to my power. But I had no choice—it was the Kingdom's honor!

"I see," she said at last in a different voice. "Very well. I promise."

"You will be discreet? And engage in no embarrassing display?"

"I promise."

"And you will stay out of his way, as much as is in your power, and never let him know what is in your heart?"

"I promise."

I exhaled slowly. "And I will hold you to it. I have sworn to do the same with Lancelot. If we break these vows, we shame ourselves, and Wales, and Britain. I know it makes the future bleak, when it should be bright. But somehow, the future must be borne."

Suddenly the day was upon us. The castle yard was filled with loaded wagons, servants scurried everywhere to fetch packages and search for last-minute, forgotten items. The troops stood by their mounts, surrounding the caravan. Goods and gifts were bundled onto pack mules. A stableboy held Zephyr's bridle in one hand and Nestor's in another, and he had his hands full. The women's litters were just behind, and from my window I saw Leonora taking charge of the women's arrangements, while Kay supervised the troops and the loading procedures. He was good at his job, patient and exacting, organized and able to keep track in his head of a thousand details. Everyone who needed information came to him, and he knew where everything was, or where it was headed, or when it would be needed, and whose responsibility it was to tend.

"Come, Guinevere," Alyse commanded. "It is time."

Lancelot appeared at the doorway and made a low obeisance to the queen. "The litters are prepared, my lady. King Pellinore is mounted and ready to be off."

"Thank you, Lancelot. We are ready. I suppose, Guinevere, you will choose to ride like a man again?"

Lancelot was shocked at her tone, but I was not. To Alyse, I was still her sister's daughter and her ward. I was not yet her Queen.

"No, madam. On this journey I shall ride in the litter with Elaine. But I should like to ride into Caer Camel when we get there."

And to everyone's surprise, I consented to be carried, while my mare walked alongside, unbridled. But I thought there might be people who would come out at crossroads to see the girl the High King had chosen to wed, and I wished to appear to them as they wished to see me. But once we got to Caer Camel, I wished to be myself. Before the people who would live with me, I wanted no false impressions. Also, to tell truth, I both dreaded and craved Lancelot's company. It was easier in the litter with Elaine, who knew my secret, than it would be riding by his side, with my face a mask and my heart in turmoil.

I was right about the people's interest in their new Queen. Not just at crossroads, but along every highway people stopped their labors and came out to watch the caravan go by. Elaine and I kept the sides of the litter open since the weather was fine, and people threw us flowers and called to us as we passed. As I got used to it, I waved to them, and they cried out their blessings and good wishes. It became a real procession, all the way through Wales, past Caerleon, across the Severn, and down into the Summer Country. Every night we stopped and set up tents, and for three hours or so received the good folk who lived round about, and accepted gifts of all kinds. I sat in a little gilded chair, with Queen Alyse on one hand, and Elaine on the other, Lancelot behind me, Bedwyr to one side, and Pellinore to the other. Kay stood at the door and let well-wishers in by twos and threes. They all brought gifts, from carved tools to woven stuffs, to trinkets to hens, vegetables and fresh eggs. One village maiden brought a yellow songbird she had trained to sing, and this caught my fancy. She kept it in a little cage of willow reeds, and it sang joyful melodies all day. Everyone who came was kind, and blessed me, and everyone seemed to go away pleased and satisfied. The farther south we went, the more people crowded to see us. Bedwyr, who was a quiet man with a shy manner, grinned at me one night as he handed me a goblet.

"My lady, you were born for this," he said proudly. "I wish Arthur could see it."

"You may be sure," Kay answered, "that he will hear about it."

Early in the mornings and very late at night I spent time with Zephyr, grooming her, crooning to her, occasionally riding her. Lancelot came with me for escort at these times, but he kept his distance. Eyes were upon us, it seemed to me.

On the tenth day we camped in sight of the signal fires of Ynys Witrin, the Isle of Glass, the Holy Hill, and knew that the next day would bring us to Caer Camel. Kay left us that night to ride on to the fortress, for he was frantic with worry that his lieutenant had not carried out his instructions, and he felt strongly that nothing should go amiss the day that Arthur's bride came to his home. Since we were so close to Caer Camel, messengers came and went constantly. The High King was still in the north, but expected well before the solstice. In his stead, I was to be welcomed by Melwas, King of the Summer Country. There was to be a ceremony, everything would be formal, stiff and endless, and I did not look forward to it. For one thing, it meant the end of Lancelot's company. For another, it meant the beginning of yet another period of preparation and waiting that would end only with the High King's arrival. All I could see ahead was one trial after another.

Hundreds of people came that night to pay their respects, and Bedwyr had to send to Caer Camel to have more carts brought up before morning to carry all the gifts the kind people brought. The people themselves truly amazed me. Arthur was a person to them, not just their war leader who kept their lands from the Saxons. He was more real to them than he was to me, and they were intensely curious about the girl he had chosen to marry. They came from every walk of life, not just lords' domains, many old and poor, some of them in good health, some in bad. Everyone wanted just a few minutes of my time, and when I saw that Bedwyr was ready to quit after three hours, I signaled him to continue. I excused Alyse and Elaine, since they were tired from the journey and wanted to rest, but I continued to see the people myself.

"My lady Guinevere," Lancelot murmured after four hours had passed, "are you not tired? Should you not take rest for tomorrow?"

"Yes, my lord, I am, and I should. But look at the people outside. Think of the distance they have come, and for what? Just to greet me and wish me good health and long life. How can I turn them away?"

Lancelot glanced at Bedwyr, who smiled and shrugged. "You can do nothing, Lancelot. It's just what Arthur would say." Lancelot nodded. The people kept coming.

The morning broke cool and cloudy, with a rose-pink haze across the sun, and the meadowlands swathed in fog. I was up early to tend Zephyr, whom I would ride today, and to have some time to myself for contemplation. I was alone in the horse lines, but people were up and about, for I heard the voices of grooms and cooks, although I could not see them. Zephyr did not like the fog, and it made her a little edgy. She moved restlessly and tossed her head while I tried to braid her mane. Then suddenly she calmed and stood quietly. My heart began to race. Lancelot's face appeared like magic in the mist across her shoulder.

"Lancelot!"

"Guinevere."

We stood and looked at each other. The longing on his face broke my heart, but there was nothing to be done.

"I came to tell you," he began, and then stopped. He cleared his throat. "How much I have enjoyed your company. I think you are the bravest woman I have ever known, and the kindest and the truest. I know you look at what is to come as a trial to be endured, but I want to assure you—Gwen, you will come to love him, as we all do. You won't be able to help it, any more than I was able to help—you know I love you, Guinevere, and I will always be at your service, whatever happens. But for Arthur's sake, we cannot—"

"Oh, Lancelot!" I whispered "It will kill me to say farewell! And I couldn't help it, either! Lancelot, I will love you till I die." I gasped as the words came out; they were the last words I had meant to say! Lancelot ducked under the mare's head and took me in his arms. Thank God the mist lay heavy around us, for he kissed me with passion, and I returned his love. Then he was gone, and I collapsed breathless against the mare's body, shaken to my soul. How the future was to be borne, I did not know. I had no protection against Lancelot.

By midmorning the mist had lifted, and the sun shone forth in splendor. Lancelot rode at my side, stone-faced and silent, wearing his sword in its ceremonial scabbard of silver set with jewels. We rode slowly, for we still had litters, and I was content to walk along, wave to the crowds who lined the road, and let the time pass. It was lovely country we rode through, rolling green hills where sheep grazed, fertile farmland, thick woods full of game. In the west from Ynys Witrin the marsh birds came in flocks, wheeling overhead and calling, and then soaring back to the Lake of Avalon. It was a rich land compared to stony Wales, soft and green and full of life.

In early afternoon Caer Camel came into view. I caught my breath at the sight of it, and Lancelot finally smiled. "There it is, Guinevere. Your new home."

There were twelve turrets, each with a flag flying gaily in the summer breeze. The castle looked huge, even from this distance, and I knew from the soldiers' talk that there was a triple ring of fortifications around it. The sandstone walls shone golden in the sun, and it looked lovely set upon its green hill. The closer we got, the steeper I realized were the sides of this hill. Only the lower shoulders were forested. Most of it was sheep meadow and open, so as to see the enemy's approach. But the fortress itself was gigantic. At one end of the flat-topped hill stood the castle, at the other a sizable woodland, all within the ring of fortifications. A city would grow there in time, although in those days there were only workmen's huts outside the castle. As we approached along the western road, we saw the great, sweeping thoroughfare that ran up to the studded double gates: the entrance to Caer Camel. This road was wide enough for ten men riding abreast, and the steep sections were paved with rough stones so the turf would never wash away in the spring rains. This was the road down which Arthur's fearful cavalry flew at a moment's notice, swooping down upon the enemy almost before he had the time to draw his sword.

"Will Merlin be there?" I asked Lancelot suddenly.

"No, my lady. Probably not."

"Why not?"

"He is old, Gwen. He has retired to a small house in the forest east of here, where he lives with an apprentice. Arthur rides out to visit him every now and again, but Merlin seldom comes to Caer Camel."

"Won't he come for the—the wedding?"

"If Arthur wants him, he will be there. But I shouldn't say it's likely."

"What has Merlin advised the King about this match?"

Lancelot eyed me warily. "It's odd that you ask. He was there when your name was proposed and said nothing. When Arthur asked him for his advice, he simply said 'what will be, will be.' No one knows how he truly feels."

I shuddered suddenly, remembering my audience with Princess Morgan. "*I* know how he feels."

Slowly the procession climbed the great roadway. Sentries saluted Lancelot, and he gave the word to open the fortress gates. Within stood King Melwas, a huge, blond man with hard, light eyes, and beside him, old white-robed Nimue of Avalon, Lady of the Lake, and Landrum, Caer Camel's Christian bishop, overdressed. A crowd of people stood behind them, and as we rode up, they broke into cheering and shouting.

Lancelot dismounted, then came around to help me down. I slid off the mare into his arms, and he recoiled as if he had been burned. We took up our positions, my hand upon his arm, and faced King Melwas. He bowed low, the Lady curtsied, the bishop nodded. They each made a speech, welcoming me to Caer Camel on King Arthur's behalf. Melwas was brief enough but the Lady went on at length, praising the Good Goddess, describing Arthur's virility and strength with a light in her eye, blessing me with fertility and talking hungrily about procreation until I began to blush. Melwas, who stood half the time staring at me open-mouthed, and the other half glaring at Lancelot, finally interrupted and brought her back to the subject at hand. I was most grateful for this. Beneath my hand, Lancelot's arm was trembling.

Then Bishop Landrum stepped forward, lavishly bedecked in gold and crimson robes, with an ornate jeweled cross hung on his breast. He began a long tirade upon the banishment of heathens and the anathema of pagan ways in a civilized land. Clearly he was enraged at the inclusion of the Lady in the welcoming ceremonies and was determined not to be outdone. But the old priestess had been included by Arthur's order, it was certain. I began to see an even-handedness here that without doubt was not shared by any of the participants.

At length, the bishop finished, and Lancelot and I both knelt to receive his blessing. Then Lancelot led me forward, followed by King Melwas and the Lady, and the bishop and Bedwyr, down the street of workmen's huts where swordsmiths, blacksmiths, armorers, coopers, carpenters, and tanners all stood outside and bowed as we went by. There was nothing there yet that was not devoted to the arts of war. At last we came to the marble steps that led to the doors of the castle. Kay was there, smiling proudly at me, and I was mightily glad to see him. As Arthur's seneschal, the castle was his domain. He thanked Lancelot formally for bringing Arthur's bride safe and virgin from Wales, and Lancelot rather stiffly replied that anything done in the High King's service was his pleasure to perform. Then Kay took me into the castle and led me to my quarters. The halls were cool and dark after the bright June sunshine, and by the time my eyes adjusted to the dim light, we were at a wide oak door carved with the Dragon of Britain and guarded by two sentries.

Beyond this door were the Queen's quarters, which had never been occupied. At long last, after many thanks and assurances, Kay left and it was over. Alyse, Elaine, and I stood in the round foyer, with Leonora, Cissa, Grannic, and Ailsa huddled by the door, and we looked about us. The place was a fighting fortress, with smooth stone walls, narrow windows, dirt floors, and stone benches. Some attempt had been made to make it fit for women. Straw was strewn across the dirt, and tapestries, touched by moth around the edges, hung on the walls.

"Well!" Alyse exclaimed. "I am glad we brought so much with us from Wales. I thought before we were burdening ourselves needlessly, but now I wonder if we brought enough."

But I found the situation amusing and rather touching. "There have been no women here. We are the first." From this central foyer branched hallways with spacious rooms. My own chambers were somewhat more elaborately furnished. There were three rooms below: two sitting rooms and a maid's chamber with wide, glazed windows that looked out upon a terrace and a lovely, walled garden. From the maid's chamber rose a stairway to my sleeping chamber. The sitting rooms were floored with colored tiles in the Roman style, depicting animals and surrounded by flowers. The walls were hung with imported carpets in rich reds and blues. Blue and gold cushions adorned plain wood benches. Someone had gone to great lengths to make these rooms habitable for women, but that someone had most definitely been a man.

Alyse began to give orders to her women as to the hangings and coverings we would need. I turned to face her. "I will give the directions as to the furnishings of my home, Alyse."

She stopped, shocked. I saw the realization sink into them all, one by one. This *was* my home now, and not theirs. Within days I would be their sovereign Queen. And one by one they sank into a curtsy, even Elaine, and last Alyse.

I went alone up the stairs into the sleeping chamber. It was a large, octagonal room, opening on a terrace, flagged in stone, that overlooked the garden. The bed was large and made of carved fruitwood, hung with silk hangings of light blue, with golden trimmings. It looked old, and the workmanship was very fine. I later learned it was Ygraine's and had come from Tintagel. It was the bed where Arthur himself was conceived and born, and where Ygraine had died. The floor tiles were blue and gold and white and covered with a soft carpet of blue, gold, and rose, so thick and rich I knew it must be one of those imported from the East. A bowl of roses sat on a slender-legged table by the window, and an old chest, made of pearwood and carved all over with flowers and vines, stood at the foot of the bed. It was a simple room, but the touches were fine; it was beautiful.

There was only one other doorway, and this was covered with a heavy leather flap. I lifted it tentatively and, hearing nothing on the other side, went in. It was another bedchamber, the twin of mine in shape and size, but plain and completely different in style and taste. The floor was polished wood, without coverings. The windows were unglazed. The bed was large, carved of some dark, shining wood I did not know, and covered with a thick blanket of stitched bearskins. There was an oak chest in one corner and a marble-topped writing table beside a triple-flamed lamp. The bed itself stood on a low dais, and on the wall at its head hung an old silk banner, much worn, of the Red Dragon of Britain clawing at a field of gold.

My heart thudded painfully in my chest, and my palms began to sweat. This was the High King's bedchamber. There could be no doubt of it. Why had I imagined that his rooms would be in another part of the castle? But they were not. This was his room, and it spoke to me about the man himself. It was a soldier's room, bare of all ornament except the banner. He wrote here, or read. He slept here, dressed here, and that was all. It was clean and quiet and calm. I went to the window. It looked west, as mine did, and in the far distance I fancied I could see the dim shadow of Ynys Witrin. Of course the King would want to be able to see the signal fires, just in case the sentry slept. Aside from the entrance to my own chamber, there was only one other door, and it led to a staircase. No doubt his chamberlain slept in the room below. I turned and walked slowly to the great bed. The bearskins were soft to my touch. I wondered about them until I recalled that his name came from "Artos," which meant "Bear." They were probably a gift. Under the bearskins the bed sheets were fine and white and clean, but not nearly so fine as the ones we had brought him. This lifted my spirits, and I looked around the room again in satisfaction. It was a restful place, and if it suited Arthur, it was a good sign.

I returned to my own chamber and sat upon the bed, thinking hard. I thought I could bear any kind of husband, even a slovenly or domineering one, provided he was fair. It would be impossible to live with a man whose respect could not be won. I was prepared to do anything the High King desired to make him think well of me and not regret his choice. If he was at all fair, the future might be endured. Somehow, seeing his room gave me hope. Next to his skill as a war leader, King Arthur was renowned for his fairness. "Arthur's justice" was a by-word for fair treatment. If so, if so, perhaps Lancelot was right, and it might not be the trial I dreaded.

But how, dear God, how was Lancelot himself to be endured?

He could not leave court—Arthur needed him—and I would die if he left. But how was I to stand it if he stayed? The utter hopelessness of it all swept over me in a wave, and at last I gave in and wept, burying my head in the cushions, sobbing like a child. I did not care. I was alone for the first time in months.

At least, I thought I was alone. But by and by I felt eyes upon me, and when I looked up, I saw a thin youth in a servant's tunic peeking in through the leather curtain.

He looked dreadfully frightened, and his eyes darted all about. He tried to look anywhere but at me.

"Is—is my lady all right?" he asked timidly. "Is there aught that I can do?"

I smiled, wiping my eyes. "There is nothing wrong that time will not heal. I am homesick."

"Ah." He plucked nervously at his shirt. "Would you care for honey mead, or perhaps wine?"

"Who are you?"

He bowed low, and kept his eyes down. "My name is Bran, my lady. I am the High King's body servant."

"If you are the King's body servant, why are you not with the King?"

He flushed hotly and stammered. "I—I—I am an apprentice, really. Varric is the chamberlain. He went with the King. I—I came up to straighten the room and set the coals in the grate. Then I heard weeping."

"Straighten the room?" I cried, incredulous. "There is nothing to straighten!" I gasped as I realized what I had revealed, as Bran looked up and grinned. I burst out laughing then, and he laughed with me. He was about my age.

"Please, Bran, apprentice chamberlain, do not tell the High King you found me weeping in here on the day of my arrival. The last thing he should have to worry about is a foolish, homesick girl."

"If I know my lord, he will understand it. I was homesick, too, when I first came here. He caught me weeping more than once."

"And what happened? Did you get a whipping?"

His jaw dropped and he stared. "A whipping? From the High King?" He did not know how to respond; clearly he took me for an idiot.

"Never mind. I see you did not. Does the High King never anger, then?"

"My lady, I have not seen it. But I have heard that he does not like his time wasted."

I smiled. "Who does? Where do you come from, Bran, and how long have you served King Arthur?"

"From Less Britain, my lady. I have been with him five years."

"You are content to stay? You don't miss your home?"

He straightened. "I wish to be nowhere else but here." Then he smiled. "You will get used to it in time. There's a lot going on. Kings and princes in and out, knights coming to offer service, knights riding out to adventures, priests and enchanters everywhere—" He stopped as I shuddered.

"And old Merlin lurking about the corridors, no doubt."

Bran looked sideways out of his eyes, and lowered his voice. "Do not let the High King hear you call him old, my lady. Merlin will not confess what it was that aged him, but the High King believes it was poison."

Now it was my turn to stare. "Surely your life will be longer if you keep such things to yourself, Bran."

"I can trust you, my lady," he said simply, with all the certainty in the world. "Would you like some mulled wine? We have a special way of making it here—"

"No, thank you, Bran. I would like a drink of water."

"I will bring you a carafe. We have a spring on Caer Camel with the sweetest water in Britain." He darted back through the curtain and then popped his head through once more.

"You might as well know, my lady. I came up here to set the room to rights because we have just had news. The High King is on his way and will arrive the day after tomorrow."

11 ❀ THE BRIDE

I had no time to be nervous. If we thought we had been busy packing, it was nothing to the unpacking. Good Kay lent us all the hands we wanted, and there was a constant flow of people, laden with furniture, hangings, cushions, and sundry necessities to and from the women's quarters. Elaine's rooms rapidly became the most luxurious, and what excess trappings she could not use, she found use for in my sitting rooms. Ailsa established herself in the small sleeping chamber at the foot of my stair. My own bedchamber I left the way I found it except for two things. I hung the singing yellow bird in its willow cage in the corner by the window, and I brought up the small carved bench that I had brought with me from Northgallis when I went to Gwynedd. It had belonged to my mother, and she had covered the bench cushion with needlework of her own design, showing the blue sea, the white stag of Northgallis, and the gray wolf of Gwynedd, with snowcapped Y Wyddfa behind. This bench I set upon the little terrace, so that I could sit there of an evening and watch the setting of the sun as I used to do on the towers of Pellinore's castle.

The rest of the castle was also thrown into an uproar by the news of Arthur's coming. The wedding gifts were all laid out, the hundreds of gifts we had collected on our journey were displayed, along with those brought by the lords and nobles who daily arrived and set up tents upon the open fields, come to see the wedding. King Pellinore's round table was set up in the dining hall, which was the only room big enough for it. All these people who flooded into Caer Camel had to be fed, and there were daily hunting parties into the woodlands for game and to the salt marshes for fowl. All the horses that carried the good folk and pulled their wagons had to be housed and tended to. All these things Kay oversaw, and although he was pressed to fuming point, he never lost his temper or said an unkind word to anyone.

Lancelot kept to the stables, which was part of his responsibility as Arthur's Master of the Horse, and with Bedwyr he drilled the guard troops daily. I saw him once or twice from Elaine's window, exercising Zephyr, and it was a rare pleasure to watch my mare's elegant paces, which I had felt but never seen. Elaine was beside herself with joy and excitement. At long last she was going to see King Arthur in the flesh. She kept pinching herself to be sure that it was not a dream. She could not decide which gown to wear when we were presented to him. I sat upon her cushioned chair and stared out her window, which faced east toward the open meadows and beyond to the wood. The meadows were alive with tents of every description, with lords and ladies from every corner of Britain. I was thankful the weather was dry for there was no mud. As it was, the meadows were so trodden down I wondered if the grass would ever come back.

"Gwen, you're not attending! I've asked you three times if I should wear the yellow or the blue."

"Wear what pleases you, Elaine."

"But what are you wearing? I don't want to wear the same."

"I don't know. I haven't given it thought."

"But you must!" She gasped. "He arrives tomorrow!"

It was an effort to turn away from the window and concentrate on clothing. "What is your mother wearing?"

"The gold." One should have expected it.

"Then wear the yellow, and I shall wear the blue. I must wear the sapphire, remember."

"Yes, and have Ailsa dress your hair with the seed pearls and bluebells again, as you did the night the Companions arrived. That was wonderful."

"There aren't any bluebells. It's June."

"Well, cornflowers then. I know I saw blue flowers in the meadows as we approached King's Gate. Send Kay to get some."

I sighed and turned back to the roiling throng that jammed the road from the valley below. "Poor Kay. I suppose I might ask Bran."

"Who's Bran?"

"The King's apprentice chamberlain."

Her eyebrows rose. "And how did you meet him?"

"Come sleep with me tonight, and I'll show you. Oh, Elaine, you will be with me tonight, won't you? Why didn't you come up to me last night?"

Elaine shook her head. "Mother forbids it. It's bad luck. The bride must sleep alone until—after you're married I can."

"But after I'm married—" I stopped, beginning to shake. The truth was, I had no idea what to expect. No one had ever spoken to me about what arrangements obtained between husband and wife. And everyone might be different. How was I to know what to do?

"I mean, when the King's away, of course," Elaine said hastily, coloring. It was too late. Arthur the man had intruded into the conversation, and we could not be comfortable with each other now. I left her shaking out the yellow gown and went to my rooms to help Ailsa unpack my wardrobe.

He came at sundown. The thundering of cavalry could be heard for miles, and I raced down from my chamber to Elaine's room and huddled with her by the window. Lancelot had troops lining the street from King's Gate, keeping back the crowds. I saw him sitting quietly on Nestor, and Bedwyr was there on his big chestnut, as twilight darkened to night. All the men had torches, and when the King came, he rode down a tunnel of light. His stallion was white and bunched his haunches to come to a sliding stop right at the castle steps. The King slid off in an easy motion as the groom stepped up to grasp the reins. He was too distant to see his features, but we could see his actions well enough. He went to Lancelot, who dismounted and saluted, but the King placed his hands upon his shoulders, said something, and then hugged him warmly.

"He is as tall as Lancelot," Elaine breathed in my ear. "But how broad his shoulders are!"

"Hush, Elaine."

He greeted Bedwyr likewise, then mounted the castle steps where Kay saluted at the door. Kay gave a long report and nodded in response to the King's questions. Then the King embraced him and slapped him on the back. He signaled to the guards, who moved to let the crowd of people into the forecourt, and they gathered at the steps. The King addressed them, but we could not hear his voice, for Elaine's window was glazed. Then the people raised a great cheer, which we heard even though the glazing, and the King turned and entered his castle. Lancelot glanced swiftly in our direction before he followed.

Elaine and I sat back and exhaled.

"Well!" Elaine exclaimed, glowing. "He's here at last! And ev-

ery inch a warrior king. You don't suppose he would call an audience tonight, do you? After we are all dressed for bed?"

"I shouldn't think so. He's been away two months. There must
be a lot to catch up on."

She raised an eyebrow. "I bet most of it's about you. He's probably grilling Lancelot right now."

I turned away, unable to bear the thought of it. "Won't you
come up with me, Elaine? Just for a while?"

"Oh, Gwen, I'd love to! Just to peek into his chamber—but
Mother would have my hide. I dare not do it. You'll be all right.
Sit with Ailsa a while and have a hot posset."

I followed her advice. Ailsa and I sat together in her anteroom,
talking about old times in Northgallis, and she sent for a warm
drink, fragrant with spices. There must have been a sleeping po-
tion in it, for soon I grew weary, and when she took me upstairs
and tucked me into the great bed, I fell asleep instantly.

I awoke quite suddenly in the night. I heard voices. I looked toward the leather curtain and saw the soft glow of lamplight
around the edges. He was there. I clutched the coverlet about my
throat and held my breath, listening. I could hear his heavy tread
on the floorboards and heard him speaking to someone, probably
Varric or Bran, but I could not hear the words. It was a warm
voice, pleasant in tone and deep. I heard muffled responses, and
quite suddenly the lamp went out, and all was quiet. I lay there
for what seemed like a long time, but I heard nothing. At last, toward dawn, I drifted back to sleep.

I awoke with sunlight streaming in through the terrace doorway.
He was gone. I rose and donned my robe, then tiptoed to the curtain.

"Bran?" I called softly, hoping it was not Varric I heard stirring
coals in the grate.

"My lady?" He came to the curtain and drew it aside. He
looked tired but, in some indefinable way, satisfied. His King was
back.

"Bran, were you up late last night?"

"Yes, my lady. We put the King to bed."

"Did—did he say anything about—"

Bran smiled. "Oh, yes, my lady. Of course he knew you had arrived safely. He got the full report from Sir Lancelot. But when
he discovered I had met you—I did not tell him I heard you
weeping, my lady. I said it was by accident."

"Oh, thank you, Bran. I am in your debt."

"Not at all, my lady. When he discovered I had met you, he asked me if I liked you."

"He did? Does he value your opinion so?"

"I could not say, my lady. But he knows that I am near your age, perhaps that was why he asked."

"What did you say?"

Bran's eyes widened. "Why, I told him the truth, of course. I said yes. He asked me why, and I told him you were without affectation. That seemed to please him."

I felt heat rise to my face. Bran looked suddenly shy and cast down his eyes, but I reached out and touched his arm. "Thank you, Bran. I think you have done me a great service."

"I told him the truth, my lady, as everyone does who knows him."

I drew back into my chamber and left him to his tasks. It boded well, that the High King was somewhat curious about me. It meant, perhaps, with luck, that he would treat me as a person. I did not want to hope too much; for if it were not so—and who could blame the High King of Britain if he had more important matters to think about than the thoughts and feelings of a girl?—I should be the more disappointed. I wondered how much Lancelot had told him. Had the King been able to see the truth behind his praise of me? I called Ailsa to me then, to occupy my mind with other thoughts.

Our audience was set for noon. People thronged all morning in the forecourt, waiting for the great doors to open. I sat with Elaine at her window, while Ailsa and Grannic dressed our hair, and watched them. Once again I noticed that people of every station were assembled, lords and ladies in fine clothes, knights and ladies-in-waiting, workmen, servants, peasants, and poor folk with only rags to wear. They all came, and they were all admitted.

Sometime later a page came to our door and brought the message that the High King was in court and waited upon our leisure. The time had come. Elaine and Ailsa put last-minute touches to my hair and gown. It was the smoke-blue gown Elaine had embroidered, and the High King's sapphire was round my neck, and Fion's earrings on my ears. Someone had gathered early cornflowers for my hair, which Ailsa dressed with seed pearls, braiding in the flowers to frame my face, and letting the long tresses hang loose down my back. In summer the sun turned my hair almost white, like a child's hair, much to my dismay. The gown itself was of heavy silk, and the day was warm, but I was shivering and my fingertips were ice.

Elaine gripped my arm, trembling. "Oh, Gwen, take care what you say! The honor of Wales is in your hands!"

As if I could forget it! With these helpful words ringing in my ears, I was led to the outer door. Lancelot was there, with Pellinore and Bedwyr, and I was never so glad to see him in my life. They led us through the long halls, where sentries snapped to attention at their posts, and slid their eyes sideways as we passed, watching. We came to the gilded doors of the Hall of Meeting and stopped. Lancelot looked down at me. My hand upon his arm trembled visibly.

"Courage, Gwen," he whispered, and I took a deep breath and stilled myself. He nodded to the guards, and the doors swung open. The babble of conversation stilled as the throng divided to let us pass, silent except for the occasional gasp and sigh. The High King's chair was on a dais at the end of the hall, and I gathered my courage and dragged my eyes off the tiles to look at him as we approached. He was standing, looking at me. It was a good face, of straight planes marked by dark brows, dark eyes, and straight lips. It was a rugged, handsome face, which one might expect of a warrior who was Uther's son. What caught me by surprise were his eyes. They were a rich, warm brown in color, glowing with a joyful light that seemed to come from within himself. He stood easily, waiting, not at all stiff or nervous, not shaking like a leaf in the winter wind, but calm and serene, and sure.

I dropped my eyes hastily and felt color rise to my face. I held on to Lancelot's arm for dear life and fought to collect my wits. The procession halted before the dais, and the High King came down the step to greet us.

"My lord Arthur," I heard Lancelot's voice dimly, "it is my pleasure to present to you the bravest, truest, loveliest maid in all Britain, Guinevere of Northgallis."

I sank helplessly into a curtsy at his feet. He extended a hand, brown from the sun, and raised me. He must have felt me shaking, for his voice was very kind.

"So this is the lass who has taken my Kingdom by storm." I glanced up quickly and saw he was smiling. "Since I left the north country, I have heard nothing but tales of your great beauty and your unflagging generosity to my people. I thank you, Guinevere of Northgallis, for this service. You are welcome here."

I tried to speak, but could not. He gently squeezed my hand and brought me to stand beside him, then turned to greet Queen Alyse and Elaine. I never heard what he said to them, for my head was whirling. His flesh was warm and dry and comforting somehow.